IT TOOK A BEAST TO TAME HER 2

TRENICE P.

It Took a Beast to Tame Her 2
Copyright © 2017 by Neicy P.
Published by Shan Presents
www.shanpresents.com

Subscribe

Text Shan to 22828 to stay up to date with new releases, sneak peeks, contest, and more....

Want to be a part of Shan Presents?

To submit your manuscript to Shan Presents, please send the first three chapters and synopsis to submissions@shanpresents.com

Previous...

Chaos

"It's funny that you should speak on family. By the way, how is yours." I spoke.

The man stared at me with fear. I don't blame him. Shit, I'd fear me too. It feels so good to be free. I have been waiting so long for this moment. I have been trapped in there forever, and I don't plan on going back. Never.

"Patience," this beautiful man spoke to me.

"Your Patience is not here at the moment. You can leave her a message. I'll make sure she gets it." I replied to him. Everyone's eyes were on me at this point. I stood and noticed that my hair was dark and longer. I flipped it and stared at the rest of the people around me. I noticed who was for me and against me.

"As I was saying, how is your family?" I asked the man again. I noticed that he had the assassin symbol on his forehead. It was the same symbol that I saw when I was little. He was there when my parents were murdered. This shall be sweet.

"Who are you? Where is Patience?" Another asked. He resembled my father. He was concerned about the turn of events.

"Who me?" I said pointing to myself. They all looked like, "*Bitch, yeah you.*"

"I am Chaos." I said, and with one wave of my hand, I sucked the life out of all my enemies. Bodies dropped, and it became silent. No birds. No crickets. Nothing.

The man and his accomplice stood paralyzed. They didn't know that they signed up for this. They thought that they were coming for some fragile ass girl. Not me. Not never.

I stilled the accomplice in his spot. He couldn't talk or move. A crystallized tree came out of nowhere and pounded him to the ground. I snapped my fingers and Felix's pack appeared. The man that killed my aunt looked at Nicole and became angry.

"If you touched them, you will regret it." he said furiously.

"A threat. You killed my parents and aunt in front of me. I think this is owed to you." I said.

"Kill all them, Lil Bit. Fuck em." I heard someone say.

"With pleasure." I closed my eyes and created the biggest water bubble. It fell over and consumed them in it. I watched as they suffered the same way me and my brothers did. The assassin was crying and trying to get in the bubble but couldn't. He started throwing air bubbles in there to create some air for them to breathe in. Clever but that won't help them. More water was placed in filling up the ones he created. When all of them were gone, the bodies dropped just like the others. I watched him cry for Nicole. His eyes turned black and he stood to charge at me. I held my hand up and he froze. I stepped closer to him and placed my index finger on his symbol. His skin started melting off his bones. We all watched until it was nothing else to see.

I turned to see that everyone was staring in shock. I was tired and ready to go to sleep.

"Patience, baby," the beauty spoke again.

"I am not her," I told him. I walked around him to get to my aunt's ashes. The wind picked up her ashes and carried them into the woods. She will be with me just like daddy and mommy.

"You are Patience. You wouldn't be here if it wasn't for Patience. Is there any way that you two can co-exist?" Xavier asked hopefully. I turned and looked him in the eyes. Something dark was calling to me. All of me. His eyes began to change, and I became weak. I was not going to give in. I did not want to be lost forever. My aunt shut me down when I lost it the first time. I started walking deeper into the woods with everyone calling my name. I vanished and was placed in front of the Guardian's facility. Someone was going to give me some answers.

Guess Who's Back

Grandpa

"These muthafuckers betta come on with my dinner." I said. I was already mad being in this bitch for so long. But, I had to do what was best for my daughters. Even though I haven't been the best father, I was trying. I gave up everything so that they can be safe. Nesida was my baby girl. Lurita was my soldier. That was how they wanted it. Lurita was a daddy's girl. She wanted to do whatever it was to make me proud. The fight between her and Nesida broke my heart. I wanted them to rule together. It didn't work out that way. That's why I was here in this confined charmed box. It was good to stand and stretch my legs to sleep. They let me out some-times since I showed no signs of breaking out.

"My Lord, your dinner. Sorry that it took so long; there was a security breach down south in the States." One of the guards said. I still had that respect on my name. No matter where I went. These fuckers knew better.

"What happened? You know I don't get signals in this bitch." I said pointing to my head. This box blocked magic in and out. They didn't know that I could break out this shit if I wanted to. They had these young ass guards on me. Little niggas didn't know shit.

"The Supreme sent the Assassins out to kill a woman. They missed her when she was a little girl but got her parents. She was being raised by her aunt. The girl came back and tried to mate with a wolf. You know that shit is forbidden. That's why they killed her parents. Anyway, the Assassins are on their way to finish the job along with the wolves." He said not paying attention.

In my heart, I knew who he was talking about. If so, I sat in this bitch this whole time and them bum ass fools killed my daughter. I broke the barrier and reached out to the world. Pain. Pain that I have never felt before hitting me hard in the chest. My babies. Both of my babies were gone.

I stood and that's when the asshole noticed the change. I let him hit the alarm and watched twenty men surround my little prison. I blinked my eyes and I was out that box.

"Hit him with everything you got!" The guard yelled.

"It won't be enough." My dark side spoked. I waved my hand and blazed three-hundred acres of land. I concentrated on my destination and was headed that way. Everybody was going to feel my pain. Every fucking last one of them.

ONE

Matteo

I remembered the first time that I held my little girls in my arms. They were both small babies. They barely made six pounds. Lurita came in the world screaming for dear life. Her eyes were big, just like her mothers. She quieted down when she saw me. I had never seen that look in the eyes of anyone. She was looking at me like I was her entire world. I rocked her back and forth, humming the same lullaby my parents used to sing to me.

Now, Nesida was different. We didn't need to hum to her because she came out quiet as a mouse. The doctors thought that she was dead. But, my baby girl was alive and well. She smiled up at her mom and began to wiggle in her arms. When I reached out to hold her, peace of no kind consumed me. Tears that I have never cried before rolled down my face. My baby had her mother's aura. Her skin was glowing, and I knew that she was going to change the world.

That was my plan. I felt that, as Guardians, we didn't need to be an equal with any other being. We were superior in every way. Humans, wolves, vamps, all those fools should have bowed down to us. But, my wife didn't see it that way. She wanted us to live in peace and harmony. That was the shit they taught her at the Guardian

1

Facility. I went there as well, but only to master Mental. I didn't plan on falling in love with one of the purest Guardians there.

Hope Locquet. She was a vision that I embedded in my memory bank. Whenever the black magic consumed me too much, I would think of my love and was brought back to my senses.

I was in my home in Lafayette, Louisiana. I sat in my library and concentrated on the events that happened the past couple of years when I was away. Scenes came and went as I watched my daughter Nesida marry and take over the Southern Territory. She was fearless and didn't take any prisoners. My baby girl did the damn thing. I had seen some of those visions before.

But, what I didn't see was the birth of my granddaughter, Patience. She was as beautiful as her mother. When I saw that her eyes began to shift into different colors, I knew that she was different. The way they kneeled at her feet as if she was royalty made me a proud Papi.

She was going to be the Queen.

Patience's father had the blood of an elder running through his veins. I still didn't approve of my daughter marrying a wolf, but she didn't give a damn of my thoughts. Nesida told me to stay away from her and their daughter. I wasn't too happy about that. I wanted to be in my grandbaby's life. I felt that I had messed up with Nesida, but I was not going to do that with Patience.

The first thing that I tried to do was help Nesida's relationship with Lurita. I told Lurita that she should have stopped holding grudges against her sister, and let that shit go. If their bond became as strong as we hoped for it to be, they would have taken over a long time ago. I didn't see Hope's vision before, because I had my own agenda. I wanted to be the darkest and the most feared Guardian alive. But, after watching my children battle each other over the years, being the darkest Guardian became unimportant. I wanted to become the father that they needed me to be. Nesida didn't believe me when I told her that I was going to change.

Change wasn't easy, though. I had made a lot of enemies. They had threatened my girls and paid dearly for it. Now that Patience was born, I didn't want her to deal with my shit when I was long gone. When the Supreme and council members called for me to be boxed, I agreed to it. But, they had to leave my babies alone. That was the deal. They promised that they wouldn't go after them and they lied.

I saw the dogs in a meeting, talking about my daughter's union with the wolf. They also talked about my grandbaby as if she was an it and not the perfect being that she was born to be. They sent them weak ass assassins after Nesida and her family. They froze her husband and killed him in front of her and Patience. Nesida lost it and went dark. The power that burst from her was something that she had never experienced. She turned them into dust with one swipe of her hand.

Nesida and Patience was the only one standing. Nesida walked in the middle of the field where there was nothing but ashes. Patience stared at her mom, and I saw that she began to change as well. Her hair was going black and her eyes were red. I couldn't believe what I was seeing.

She was the Supreme of Light and Dark. The Queen of the Guardians. There were only Supremes of the Light that were leaders of the Guardian Facilities. We had a couple of Dark Lords out there, but they didn't practice like the others. If they were caught practice dark magic, they would have been sentenced to death.

Patience was standing there with more control over her power than Nesida. Nesida began to consume too much and perished right before the eyes of her daughter. Patience began to get irritated and lost control, until Lurita stepped in. Lurita came in as her dark being, prepared for a fight.

"Calm down little one before you destroy yourself." She said in an uncertain voice.

Patience stared at her and continued to suck in the power that her mother had released. She then turned and walked to her deceased father and turned his body into ashes. She picked them up and pulled the ashes to her mouth. She whispered something to it and let it go. The ashes drifted into the night air and landed in the middle of the woods. Patience turned to face Lurita. The face that she made scared the shit out of her Aunt. It looked like that fight that Lurita didn't want was something she was about to get. Patience threw an electric ball at Lurita that hit her in the chest. It was so powerful that it knocked the darkness out of her. Lurita struggled getting up and tried to approach Patience another way.

"Little Angel, if you don't want to hurt your brothers, this needs to stop. Think of them and your cousins. What about Xavier? Think of him, Angel." She said calmer. Hearing that she was going to hurt her brothers and this Xavier boy had her shifting back into that sweet little girl. I was able to see the darkness lingering but she was more stable now.

Lurita approached her and chanted a spell that put Patience out. She picked her up and vanished into thin air. I watched Lurita raise Patience to be the young woman that she was now. She had a couple of incidents that needed to be covered but Lurita did an excellent job. I was proud of my daughter. When I asked for peace between the two, Lurita was against it. She was just like me and saw the world as hers. That was all my doing and I apologized to her for that. I never wanted to be the reason for my daughter's downfall.

I skipped through some of the events that brought my granddaughter back to Louisiana. She met up with the wolves and her intended mate. He looked to be different than the others. I couldn't put my finger on it until his mother confessed her Guardian ancestry. The prophecy was looking to be fulfilled by my granddaughter. I noticed how she was struggling with surrendering herself to the Alpha. She also had Alpha and Elder blood in her. It was hard for two Alphas to be in the same space. I gotta give it to Xavier; he shut that shit down at the door.

Lurita started training baby girl on how to use her magic and not consume it. Their bond became stronger than before. Lurita stood by her every step of the way. But, what I didn't understand was why Lurita was training her that way. She knew Patience's potential. I closed my eyes to give myself a break for a minute. It was so much that I had missed, trying to protect my daughters. In the end, I made it easier for them bastards to kill them.

I blamed myself for their deaths.

I sat up and went back into the visions. Lurita was battling the Guardians and protecting Patience at the same time. They got the best of her when she was trying to send Patience back into the house she spelled. After witnessing her Aunt's death, she transformed. The power that came from her was unbelievable. I didn't understand the shit. She could have done this in the beginning to save Lurita. I became angrier as I watched my daughter gasp for her last breath when all this shit could have been prevented. Not only Lurita but Nesida could have been saved as well if Patience would have unleashed her power. My grandbaby was the one to fear. Her magic already surpassed mine. This shit was hard to swallow.

I got up and blew a hole in the wall. I needed to calm down if I was going to make this shit work. I gotta keep myself in check.

Patience

"Shit," I said, squinting my eyes open. I was laying on the ground, next to some burnt stuff. The sun was covered with smoke in the air. I sat up and looked around. My jaw dropped. I got off the ground and began to stare at the scene before me. There was debris, blood, and bodies everywhere. I took a step back and almost tripped over a body that looked like it was mauled to death. This shit was crazy. I looked down in horror.

"Oh my God." I whispered. I didn't know where I was, and I was surrounded by dead bodies. "Please God, don't let this be my family," I asked.

I started reaching out to Xavier and Dom. They were feeling worried and scared. Good. I was happy that they were ok, but why were they worried? I looked around and noticed that I was far away from home. I walked over bodies that looked like they were bitten and then set on fire. Who could have done something like this? I saw a sign laying on the ground next to a scorched cloak. I walked over to read it. I hoped that it could have given me a clue of where I was. When I got to it, it read "Southern Guardian Facility."

What the fuck? I looked around and didn't see a facility. I looked back at the sign to see if that was what it said. But, my reflection caught me off guard. I had blood all over my face. I raised my hand up to wipe it off but saw that my hands were covered in blood as well. I backed up, now afraid of my own reflection.

"No, oh my God, no. What have I done?" I looked around again to see how much damage was really done. Acres and acres of land was destroyed.

There was something that looked like an obstacle course for the Guardians that were in training, covered with chairs, tables, and burnt books. Wheels of cars and other shit was spread out all over. I felt that it became harder to breathe, when I saw pieces of cribs and a child's doll.

"This can't be happening," I said before I turned and ran into the woods.

I had to get away from that scene. I tried to think of home, so that I can teleport there. But, the way my emotions were going created storm clouds with heavy rain pouring out of them. I came up to a lake and without hesitation I jumped in. I scrubbed the blood off my body and tried to erase what I just witnessed. Lightening and thunder began to hit the trees and knocked them out of the ground. I didn't care. I wanted to go home. I needed to feel safe again.

I got out of the lake and sat on one of the fallen trees. Was I capable of doing some "Werewolf in London," type of shit like this? My throat and stomach began to burn. I leaned over and emptied out everything that I ate. I closed my eyes at the sight. My answer was in the evidence on the ground.

"Fuck," I screamed out. "I gotta get home."

I sat up and tried to focus. I had to calm myself down, because the thunderstorm was getting worst with my emotions. I took a deep breath and relaxed. I didn't want my family to see me like this. So, I thought of another place that I wanted to appear. I had enough energy to teleport myself where I needed to be. I sat back and opened my eyes. I was in the tree that I healed when I was on the trail with the girls. I pulled my knees to my chest and began to cry.

My Aunt Lurita wasn't here anymore. My crazy ass Aunt. I knew that she loved me, but to hear it with her last dying breath, made me feel so helpless. I wish that I could have done more to save her. Everyone was talking about this great power I had, but where was it when I needed it the most. It was probably at the Guardian facility roasting and eating people. How can I explain that to anyone without sounding so…monstrous?

I hoped that they will forgive me. Since I came back into their lives, I have been causing nothing but trouble. I knew that the Guardians were going to come after me, for destroying their facility and the Guardians that were in it. I didn't want to put my family in no more danger. I thought that it would be best if I just stayed away. I leaned back and rested my head on the tree. I just needed time. Time to mourn the loss of my Aunt and myself. After what I saw, I knew in my heart that I will never be the same Patience again.

TWO

Xavier

———————

"What the fuck just happened?" Xander asks no one in particular. Everyone saw what happened and was shocked at the event that they'd just witnessed. I was concentrating on reaching out to Patience's mind. I had no luck, while my brothers started panicking.

"Fuck all that bullshit. Where the fuck is my sister?" Maxi yelled.

"I don't fucking know, Maxi. I have been standing here just like the rest of us. I don't know who the hell she has become. The bitch took my Queen." I shouted out to Maxi. I was pissed off that I couldn't feel her, and Maxi wasn't making the shit better with his ranting.

"I am trying to reach out to her, but her mind feels like it is closed off." Nick said. We all tried to reach out and was hit with a striking pain.

"Shit," I grabbed my head like the others.

"Did she just do that?" Josh asked in pain.

"This bitch is crazy." Maxi added. "We gotta get her out of my sister man, before she does something that we all may regret." My mom walked up to us and told us to go in the house. "I'm not going into that house Ma. I gotta find my Queen." I told her. I turned to walk further into the woods. She couldn't have gone too far, hopefully.

"You won't find her, Xavier, until you listen." My mother yelled. I turned to face her. "Chaos is created by the dark magic inside of Patience. You have to reach her from your Guardian side Xavier. Chaos doesn't see herself ass wolf." She turned and ran towards the house. I tried to focus on my Queen and I felt a piece of her. My mom came back and gave me a picture. "This is a picture of the closest Guardian's facility. She is seeking revenge. This would be the first place that she would go to for that."

"He doesn't possess that type of magic, Noel." Elder Nico walked up and said to her. The other Elders were looking shocked as shit. Nico was the only one that didn't look surprised at what we had all just witnessed. I walked up to him with a glare.

"What do you know?" I asked him.

"It is not the time to discuss that. We have to find Queen first. I will explain only when she is present." He sternly said.

"Xavier, try to reach her through your Guardian side." Dom asked again.

"I don't know how to do that shit. I always thought it was my wolf that was communicating with her." I said. I turned towards my mom and asked if there was anything else that I could do to find her. I felt that she needed me. Not in a protecting way, but for support.

"That is the only way, Xavier. If you can't, you will have to wait for Chaos to release her." My mom said, sadly. And I understood why. There was a chance that Chaos won't let Queen out.

"I can't just sit here and do nothing." I said.

"I'm going with you." Nick added, as he turned to the other guys. "Clean up this mess. Treasure, Cam, and a couple of others are coming to check on our wounded. Make sure they have every-thing they need."

"The other pack members can do that Nick. Let us come with y'all. We can cover more ground like that." Maxi said. You could tell that besides me, he was worried the most out of the brothers.

"Same here, X." Xander agreed. "I can't go home and tell my

mate that I lost her sister. That will kill her." He told me. He stood in front of me and Nick, with the rest of our brothers as they waited for instructions.

"Alright. Xavion, go east. Xander, go south of the station. She loves the woods back there. I will go check around our home. Nick, you should check around your house. Maxi and Josh, try to look in a place she was more comfortable around. She doesn't know these areas as good as we do. So, she would go to a place that she is familiar with. If any of you finds her, let me know." I told them.

"Yes, you guys go on and find her. We will take care of everything here." Elder Locklear said.

I turned and ran into the woods. My bones started shifting and my fur came out, in a mid-jump. All of my senses became stronger. I heard my brothers shifting with the same thoughts as mine. I felt someone else behind me and saw that it was Elder Nico in wolf form. What the fuck was he doing?

"*I told you that I will explain when we get the Queen back.*" He told me telepathically.

I ignored him and continued running towards my home. I didn't feel her presence near, but I had to start somewhere. We were all looking for three hours with no luck of finding her. I went to the station and met up with the rest of them. Nick and his brothers were pacing with mine. Elder Nico was just sitting on the steps. "Is there any way that she transported herself to Texas. Maybe she wanted to go to a place that held the memories of her Aunt." Josh said.

"That is a good idea. Xander, can you ask Jess if someone can pass over there to check that out." I asked him.

He let out a sigh and nodded. I knew that he would have to go through hell explaining this to Jess. But, we had to try something. I was getting desperate at this point. She was out there by herself with that crazy bitch controlling her. The magic that she exuded during the battle was a sight to see. I was used to Guardians chanting with their spells and shit. But, she didn't chant. It just came out of her without being provoked.

"Mom said that Chaos was looking for revenge, right? Is there any way that we can get in touch with their facility to see if they saw her?" Xavion asked.

"No. I don't want them to be looking out for her. They sent assassins for her. If they think that she was about to walk in their front door, the Guardians will prepare themselves for an attack. I don't want to give them bitches a heads up on that." I told him.

Xander walked over to us after he made the call to Jess. "She is calling the neighbors around the house right now to knock on the door."

"Good," I said, thinking of other ways to reach her. I was not going to rest until I get my Queen back. I was thinking of any other places that she may have gone to. She told me that New Orleans was another place that she felt free in. We had many houses out there, but we only went to one. I was about to suggest that, but was hit with sadness, sorrow, and so much pain.

"Fuck," I said, jumping to my feet. "Do you feel that, Nick?"

"Hell yeah." He replied. "She is close." Without another word, we all shifted and headed in the direction of our Queen. She was sad and hurting. I hoped whatever happened within those hours that she was missing, didn't cause her physical harm. We ran and ran until we came up to a big ass glass looking tree. We all shifted back on two legs and walked up to it cautiously.

"This is where I met her and her friends at. They were standing at this tree, when Nicole Crystal approached them." Maxi said. We were all looking up at it with amazement. The tree branches were pulled up to the sky. It looked like it was holding or protecting someone in it. I reached out my hand to touch it and it was warm.

"Queen, are you in there?" I asked as calmly as possible. I wanted to rip the branches off, but thought about the first time I kicked the tree that she was in. We couldn't have climbed it because of the smooth texture.

"Lil Bit, answer us. Are you in there? Are you hurt?" Nick asked with concern in his voice.

When we didn't get a response, we began to worry. What if she was hurting too bad to respond? Shit. "Queen. Baby, please answer me. I need for you to be ok. Please, Queen." My voice cracked a little bit. My emotions were high as shit. Xavion walked up to me and grabbed my shoulder. "She is good, X. You got to believe that." He said.

We all looked up when the branches started bending downwards. We all stepped back in surprise. I have never seen anything like this before. And the way that everyone else was looking, I guessed that they thought the same. One of the branches stretched out in front of me. I placed my feet on it to try it out.

"It's good." I let Nick know. I took a step on it and began walking up. Nick was behind me while the others stayed on the ground. When I got to the top, I saw my Queen sitting up, with her legs pulled to her chest.

"Queen," I called out softly. Her head came up slowly with her eyes closed. Queen's hair was her original color. Chaos' hair was black, and eyes were red. I was hoping to see those pretty brown eyes that kept me in a trance when I looked into them. She opened her eyes and they were brown, but full of grief and misery. I was in front of her in three strides. I picked her up and pulled her into my body. I held onto her tightly, as she cried.

Nick came over and placed his hand on top of her head. "You are ok, Lil Bit. We are here. We all are."

She continued crying in my arms. There was nothing like feeling the pain that your mate felt. I was ready to rip the heads off all the muthafuckers that ever caused her the pain. I walked back down with her in my arms, to where the others were waiting. Everyone came up to us and placed their hands on her. "I am going to get her home. Take care of everything else." I told them.

"You got that, bruh. Just take care of my sister." Nick said.

"Will do," I said and turned in the direction of my house. Elder Nico started following me. I shook my head, not wanting to deal with his shit right now. "Not right, man. Take yo ass somewhere else. We can have that discussion later."

"That is fine, Xavier. But, I am here to protect the Queen. Nothing more." He told me. I felt myself getting angry. Was he suggesting that I couldn't protect her? He must have felt what I was feeling because he came back with something else after that. "It is a story that the Queen needs to be well enough to hear. And we can see that she is not well enough yet. Don't let your ego push yourself in a battle that you know nothing about, Alpha." He told me.

Right now, he was right. My focus needed to be on Queen. I continued walking without a backwards glance. When I got her home, I carried her straight to the bathroom. We soaked in silenced. After bathing her and myself, we crawled into the bed and went to sleep.

~

I have been home with my Queen for a couple days now, and she still wasn't talking. I asked her questions about random shit and she hunches her shoulder in response. Nick and her brothers had been calling to come by. Maybe she needed the whole family to be here with her. I wasn't above asking for help from the family, especially when it came to my Queen. I called up Nick and the rest of the family to pass by. Jess was out with Tori and Loreen. They had been out of their mind worried. Jess went to distract them and told me that, no matter what, they were coming by tomorrow to check on her.

She was standing by the island when I walked into the kitchen. She had her hair pulled up in a messy ponytail, with my shirt on and a pair of leggings. I walked over to her and grabbed her by the waist. "Good morning, Queen. How did you sleep?" I asked, while I stared into her eyes. They weren't the same. I didn't see the woman that was usually in them.

"I slept ok." She spoked for the first time since we got home. I was relieved that she responded. Even if she was lying to me.

"Ok, well everyone is coming over to see you. Jess and your girls are coming over tomorrow. I have some things that I need to take care of at the station. But, if you need me here or think that it's too soon, I will call and cancel all this shit. Just say the word Queen." I told her. She was my main concern. If people feelings got hurt to make her happy, oh fucking well. I was craving to see a smile on my baby's face.

"No, Alpha. I'm good. I know that you have other things to take care of. I'm ok. Just trying to bounce back, but it's harder than I thought." She said with a sigh. "Maybe being around the rest of the family will help."

"Yeah, Queen, it should. We are here." I said and kissed her on them soft ass lips. I was trying to be sensitive to her feeling, but I needed her in the worst way. I picked her up and placed her on top of the island. "I miss you, Queen." I told her kissing on her neck. She moaned out my name and I was ready to take her ass right there. Someone cleared their throat to get our attention. I dropped my head back and wanted to fuck him up. "Is there a reason for you to be here, Elder Nico." I asked him while trying to calm myself down.

He had been around since we got home. He never came in the house, though. "The door was open, Alpha, and the rest of the gang is waiting in the family room." He replied.

I looked back at my Queen and she was smiling. It didn't reach up to her eyes the way it used to, but it'll do. "Later," I promised.

"Sooner," she said and nipped at my bottom lip. She pushed me back and jumped off the island. Queen got to the door and turned towards me.

"What's wrong?' I asked.

"I don't know what to tell them." She said all nervous and shit.

"You don't have to tell them a goddamn thing. And nobody is here to judge you. They just wanted to see how you are doing." I said and walked up to her. I grabbed her face and kissed her once again. I have been doing that shit a lot. "Relax." She nodded her head and took my hand into hers. I pushed the door opened and walked out with Elder Nico following. This muthafucker was like a guard dog fa real.

We walked into the room and everyone stood up. No one really knew what to say. They didn't want to set her off and have her disappearing on us again. She was just as nervous. Her hand was trembling in mine. I gave her a slight squeeze to remind her of the conversation that we just had in the kitchen.

"Lil Bit, are you ok? I mean, you are our Lil Bit, right?" Maxi said approaching her with caution. You can tell that she didn't know what was going on. Everyone was looking at her waiting for her to respond. She looked up at me, confused by the questions. I pulled her to me and kissed her forehead.

"Yes, this is Lil Bit, my Queen." Everyone exhaled the deep breath that they were holding. Nick came towards us, took her out of my arms, and pulled her into a bear hug.

"Damn it, Lil Bit, don't ever do nothing like that again. I am not afraid to admit that you had me worried as shit." He said after he pulled back from her.

"Sorry Dom, I didn't mean to worry you. Any of you." She said almost in tears.

"It's ok, Lil Bit. I'm just happy that you are here with us now." Josh said and pulled her into a hug.

"Yeah, even though Xavier was holding you hostage and Elder Nico didn't let me pass the gate." Maxi said. He was eyeing Elder Nico like he was ready for him to deny it. We all looked at him and he gave us a blank expression. We really had to get his story.

Maxi grabbed Queen and held onto her tight. "You can't leave me like that again. We just got you back. I don't know what I would have done if we didn't find you."

"Let's not think about the "what-ifs". I'm here now, that's all that matters." She told everybody. Maxi kissed her on the forehead and released her to greet the rest of the family.

Xavion and Xander held in what they wanted to say, and just hugged her. Treasure, Cam, and my mom grabbed her in a group hug and started crying. You can see that this was something that she needed. I knew that losing her Aunt made her feel that she was all alone. Hopefully, feeling the emotions of the people around was going to change that. Everyone took a seat and Queen walked over to me.

"Where the fuck did you get all that power from, Lil Bit?" Maxi asked her the question that we all wanted to know.

"What power are you talking about, Maxi?" She asked suspiciously.

I came up behind her and wrapped my arms around her waist.

"What do you remember about the battle that happened by my mom, Queen?"

"I remember feeling pain in my back. Elder Nico was trying to stop me from going outside but I had threatened him. When I went outside, I saw that you were on the ground with a knife of some sort in you back. I pulled the pain out of you and the magic that was surrounding the wolves. I saw my Aunt Lurita fighting three Guardians. I knock one of them out with the energy ball. Then Aunt Lurita," she said in a whisper and stopped talking.

I was watching the memories replay in her head. She was watching her Aunt Lurita get blasted with some dark ass ball and dying. The pain that she felt was coming back and she was slipping back to her unconscious state. Queen was consuming too much energy at one time. I tried to balance it but was pushed out of her mind and was hit with the same pain as before. She began to transform back into her grandfather's dark power. Her hair was changing black, and I didn't have to see her eyes. I knew that they were red and full of hate.

Chaos removed my arm from around her waist and blasted me through the wall. My brothers tried to calm her, but they got stilled to the spot. Treasure walked up to Chaos and tried to talk to her. I thought she was getting through, but she grabbed her by the neck and tossed her to the side. Dom shifted into his wolf and attacked her. His wolf was going for her throat. Chaos smiled and taunted him with kissing sounds.

I came through the door and saw Nick's position over Chaos. I knew what she was able to do, but I would never think of her as a threat. My wolf reacted, and I shifted. I charged at Dom and we began to fight. We were snapping at each other's neck. I didn't want to hurt my brother because I knew that he was only protecting his mate. I couldn't let him do that shit to my Queen, though.

THREE

Patience
___

*W*hat the fuck?

I was sitting here, telling them about what I remembered. And in a blink of an eye, these muthafuckers was up in here fighting. The men stood around and watched, while Cam cradled an unconscious Treasure. Holy shit, what just happened? I stepped in and tried to stop them from fighting. Maxi grabbed me to step back.

"Don't interfere Lil Bit." He demanded me.

"Stop this shit, Maxi. Xavion, why y'all just standing there watching this shit." I yelled.

"You don't step in a fight between two Alphas." Xander said to me in a clipped tone.

I stepped back and went to check on Treasure. Camryn held onto her tightly and a growl escaped her throat. I stopped moving with my hands up. She was looking at me with fury in her eyes and showing me her lengthened teeth. I turned and watched my brother and Alpha fight. The shit started making sense. The only reason why Xavier would attack Dom, is if Dom would attack me. The only reason for that, is if I attacked Treasure.

"Shit," I said to myself. I looked down at Camryn and asked the question that I already knew the answer to. "Cam...did I do this?" Her eyes became softer before she nodded her head. I took a step forward and kneeled in front of them. I didn't know what I had done, but I had to make it right.

Treasure was still unresponsive. I placed my hand on top of her head and chanted. Treasure's eyes opened slowly. "Hey sis," I said with tears in my eyes. I never wanted to hurt my family. This other part of me has been released and is trying to take control over me. That was what my Aunt Lurita didn't want. She told me that my mother couldn't control such power because she has always denied that side of herself.

I had to find a way for us to coexist or I was going to die, just like my mom. Treasure looked up to me and wiped the tears from my eyes. "It's ok, Lil Bit. Sisters fight all the time." She said with a smile. She was trying to comfort me, through her own discomfort. I hugged her, and she told me repeatedly that it was ok.

We got up and saw that the Alphas were now done fighting, but all eyes were blazing at me. "I am sorry you guys. I will try my hardest to control this other side of me. I just don't know what to do now that my Aunt Lurita is gone." I said getting sadder. Xavier walked towards me with the frown on his face and grabbed me.

"You better get her under control or I will." Xavier said with a lot of tension. He was threatening her, and I was all for it. I didn't know how we were going to do that, but it had to be done. He wrapped his arms around me and pulled me to him.

"For real Lil Bit. I almost ripped your throat out for attacking Treasure." Dom said, while going to Treasure. He picked her up and carried her to the couch.

"I know, Dom, and I am truly sorry." I said with the tears again. I didn't want to lose my family because of this out of control bitch. I still couldn't tell Xavier about what I woke up to at the facility.

"We will have to avoid hitting triggers that will bring her out. We know that reliving my aunt's death is one. Our parent's death is another trigger. If we can stay away from any of those emotional events, maybe that would give me the time I need to control her." I said to the only family I had left. I couldn't believe that my aunt was dead. I felt myself slipping again a little. I tried to remain on the forefront, but she was feeding on my emotions that I was bottling in.

"Don't let her win, Lil Bit. Fight that shit." Josh spoked.

He was worried. They all were.

I had to fight for them. Xavier's grip on me became tighter and everyone backed up. Josh and Maxi stood there with Xavier. My vision gets blurry and all black is the last thing I saw.

~

"Concentrate Angel it is not that hard for you to control this power. You are stronger than you think." My mother told me. She was teaching me a way to use the strength and stamina of my wolf, to enhance my Guardian powers. I was drenched with sweat. I tried my hardest, but I still couldn't figure this out. I wanted to go outside and play with my brothers. I didn't want to do this.

"Mom, I can't do it." I said pouting.

"You can't, or you don't want to." She said sternly. I usually didn't hear this tone from my mother. She was frustrated because I wasn't into it and lying to her. My mother and father were always talking to us about our abilities. They told us that they were hard on us because they knew our potential. She was right. I didn't want to.

"I don't want to, Momma. I want to go outside and play with my brothers." I said truthfully. She glared at me and then steadied her look.

"What would happen if you were playing with your brothers and your power comes out because they do something to make you angry. But, at this point, you can't control your magic. They get hurt and there is no way to reverse your actions. What would happen then?" She asked.

"You can reverse it. I saw you bring the life to the earth." I said angrily. I couldn't believe she would let my brothers die to prove a point.

"I can't reverse your magic Patience. Your magic surpasses mine. Even now."

"You are a liar!" I screamed out as a black ball flew from my body and went at my mom. She dodged it and boosted upwards. She floated in the air with her golden hair shining brightly. I was far from scared. I wanted to know why she wouldn't revive my brothers.

"Calm yourself Angel." She said calmly.

"No, tell me why you wouldn't save my brothers." Another black mass came from my body. I was crying and upset at this whole situation. My mother knew how much I loved my brothers. To put them in a scenario with the possibility of me hurting them, and she not help them, was cruel.

My mother turned back to herself and shook her head.

"Patience, it's not that I won't help them. I can't help them. When I bring back life to the earth, it's only because it was damaged by the humans of the world. That sweetheart is an easy fix for me. Magic don't harm the life of the earth, people do. That is why I am training you to control your powers so that nothing like that would have to be reversed. Your powers, Angel, are something I have never seen before. You have to learn to control and live with it or you will kill the ones around you." She said sadly. I calmed down and collapsed because of all the energy that was used to create the black masses. My mother came and picked me up.

"Oh, Angel, I would never intentionally watch my boys die. I love them like they are my own. Never say anything like that again. Promise."

"I promise. I'm sorry mommy." I said with the tears and tiredness in my voice.

"It's okay, Angel. I'm happy to know that you'll go above and beyond to protect your brothers. You are truly your father's fierce daughter." She said to me with a chuckle. "Get some rest. We will continue later."

I woke up drenched in sweat. I sat up in the bed and cradled my head in my hands. Shit, I was a fucked-up kid. I replayed the dream over and over in my head. My mother knew about this power. She had been trying to train me for this shit. Now that my aunt was gone, there was no one I trusted enough to help me. I turned my head when a presence was felt in the room. Xavier was sitting there watching me like a hawk in wolf's eyes. He was elbows were on his knees and he was leaning forward with his dreads hanging in his face. His caramel skin looked smooth to touch. He was sporting a five o'clock shadow, which looked sexy on him. I stood to walk closer to him and his eyes never left mine. He was studying me. Ole' girl had been popping up, with no warnings, tearing shit up. The worse part about everything was, I couldn't promise them that the shit would never happen again.

"Are you alright?"" Xavier asked me as I got closer. He said it with no feelings.

"Yeah, I'm good." I told him softly. He got up and brushed past me towards the door. I called out to him and he continued walking. What the fuck was his problem? I grabbed his arm and he snatched it away from me.

"What the hell is wrong with you?" I asked now getting upset.

"You can pretend to not have control over your darker half if you want to, but I'm not buying it. I know how strong you are, Queen. The power I felt when you sucked that pain out of me, was something I have never felt or seen before. Chaos can't have the power she possesses, unless you give it to her. Stop feeding her that shit and take control the way you are meant to do." He said and walked out the door.

I was pissed for a minute, until I thought about what he said. It was the same shit my aunt and mother told me. I was able to feel the power. I just couldn't channel it to go where it needed to be. I needed to find someone who understood this shit before I hurt my family.

FOUR

Xavier

$\mathscr{I}$ was about to fuck something up for real. The constant challenge from Queen was driving me crazy. If other muthafuckers see how she acted towards me, outside of our home, I was going to get challenged. Not only for my spot on the board, but as an Alpha to my pack and to her. Elder Nico was watching over her while I was away. He thought that she needed to be guarded when I was away.

I agreed, cuz I had to get this shit together or I was going to lose everything.

My mother was a Guardian before. She wanted to marry my dad with no issues, therefore she had to will her powers to me. I knew that I was different from my brothers. I was stronger, faster, and I was able to vanish into thin air. I thought it had something to do with me being a mate to a powerful Guardian.

That was never the case though.

I didn't know the history of my mom's family. I was on my way over there to have a sit-down with her. I called Dom and the rest of the guys to be there for this conversation. I needed all the help that I can get and maybe, we can help Queen with whatever is going on with her. She wiped out at least forty Guardians with one move in the fight in front of my mother's house.

We were all surprised and thankful that she took them out. What we didn't know was that she had turned dark. When she turned to look at me with bleak eyes, I knew that my Queen was gone. I couldn't believe that a woman that cherished life the way she did, was capable of that. We all understood why her Aunt Lurita erased that part of her memory. Chaos, as she called herself, was out of control. The attack on the family was proof enough.

The Elders didn't want to mate us yet. They told us that we had to continue with our premarital meetings. I didn't care how crazy my Queen was. Her crazy was my crazy and I wasn't letting her go. I was the only one that was going to claim her. My beast already claimed her. I was waiting for her to finish with the claiming.

I pulled up to my mom's house and it looked brand new. The house had a fresh coat of a bright ass yellow paint on it. The flowers were blooming, and the lawn was freshly cut. Xavion and Xander had been working hard to get our mother's house back to the way it was before the battle. The wraparound porch was white with a swing by the floor to ceiling window. I stepped onto the porch as Xavion was walking out the house.

"How is she," he asked while holding a glass of lemonade. My brothers were very worried about their Queen. They all saw her as family before I started having feelings towards her.

"She's good. She just got to get a handle on her darker side before I fuck her up." I said getting angry all over again.

Xavion laughed along with Xander, who was walking around the porch. "Yeah right. Chaos will kick yo ass. We all was there when she blasted yo ass through the wall. You don't have to front, Xavier. Queen is bad, and you like that shit."

"Fuck you, Xander. That shit was far from funny. She also attacked Treasure and that shit had Nick's teeth around her neck." I said, bringing in the reality of the situation.

"Yeah, we saw that too. What are you going to do?" Xavion asked sobering up.

"I don't know. I am here to talk to mom about this magic that I have. Hopefully, I can help her through this shit. Why don't y'all come and sit in this conversation? It can be something that we all can learn from." I told them walking inside the house. Her house was an open concept. The family room was to your left and the living room was on your right. There were the stairs and the kitchen straight ahead with the office door further down. Mom was in her apron cooking as usual. I walked towards the kitchen to greet her.

"Hey mom, you got a minute." I asked her while grabbing the warm rolls she took out the oven. I didn't know why we ate that shit when we knew it was hot.

"Sure baby. Dinner is almost ready. I made some soup for you to bring back to Patience." She said to me as she wiped her hands on the apron.

"I hope you made enough fa us Nanny." Nick said, walking in with Josh and Maxi.

"Na, you know I made enough for all of y'all. I have containers for Camryn and Treasure." She told him.

"Thanks Nanny, cuz Treasure and Camryn been cooking some weird sh-stuff lately. I have been eating out every night. Nick and Josh sit there and that sh-stuff." Maxi told her.

Josh looked at him with a frown. "That sh-stuff be good. I don't know what you are talking about."

"What type of stuff does she cook?" I asked them curiously.

"Corn and rice. Pork chops, fried or baked chicken and some other things." He said as he stuffed another roll and a spoonful of beef stew my mom made in his mouth.

"Ain't nothing wrong with that," Xander told him. "You exaggerating as usually."

"Bacon," he said and continued eating like we were supposed to understand that shit.

"What the fu-hell," Xavion said, catching himself like everybody else. Mom didn't mind us cussing. We sometimes slipped up and do so when we are mad. But, we didn't randomly cuss around her.

"They cook everything in bacon grease." Maxi said with an involuntary shake. "I would never look at bacon the same again." We all started laughing.

"Shut yo stupid ass up. I'm gonna tell Treasure and Cam you were over here talking about their cooking. They goin eff you up and I am not helping." Nick said to Maxi.

"Me either," Josh said.

"Wait a minute. Treasure is pregnant." Ma asked.

Nick nodded his head with pride. "Aww man, congrads." I told Nick and put my hand out to shake his. Nick reached out and grabbed it.

"Thanks brother." He replied.

"That's crazy, man." Xavion said and then shook his head. "Speaking of crazy, how about Nicole Crystal and that Guardian assassin? They were trying to marry her off to you, but she was fu- messing with his ass. What was all that about?"

"Fa real, they some hoes fa that. They were knocking my daddy fa being with Nesida and his hoe ass daughter was over there fucking this punk ass broom rider. I was about to fu- Ayye! What the FU-" Maxi yelled out after Josh punched him in the chest. We were all staring at this fool like he lost his fucking mind. Clearly, he forgot that my mom was in the room. He looked up and understood why he got hit. "Oh, I'm sorry Nanny."

"Boy, you alright. I know that you are upset about what's going on. It's not like I haven't heard it before." Mom said as she stood and we all sat at the oversized kitchen island. We all waited for mom to start talking again. I had a lot of questions, but I wanted her to start with whatever she thought was necessary.

I guess she was waiting on me, when she told me, "Tell me what you want to know, Xavier. I don't have time to guess what's going on in your head."

"What happened to your family Ma?" I asked.

"My family was against me marrying your father. I didn't want or need their approval. I felt that Jacob was the right man for me. I didn't care that he was a wolf. Love was love, and I was in love with him. My parents banished me from the family. When I surrendered my power to you, my father and brother came to claim you as a Vandis. That was my maiden name of course. But, your father ran them off. He told them if they were to ever return, he was going to rip their throats out. They told me that we will pay for not giving you up. I wasn't worried because you guys know how your father can get." We all laughed. My father can be a bit much when it came to us.

"When you consumed my magic, it became stronger than what I was ever used to. Your wolf and the blood of the Elder enhanced that magic. You developed some abilities that I never had as a Guardian. My family bloodline is not of the strongest Guardians. That was why my father and brother came to get you. They thought that they can use you for their own personal gain. You were going to be offered to one of the royal Guardian families." She told us, while shaking her head.

"We started receiving gifts and money from the Patterson family. Your father sent the shit back with a big "fuck you" and have a nice life letter. Jackson was ready to get involved as well. Nesida stopped them from going to their residents. She went and talked to them, and they stopped sending things and contacting us any further."

"What type of power did you have, Mom?" Xander asked. It was good that they were here. I was getting pissed off at the shit my mother was saying and couldn't find my voice to ask shit.

"It is not a power, Xander. It's magic and there are three types of magic that the Guardians have. Elemental, which controls all of the elements: water, earth, air, fire, and lighting. You also have Mental magic, which is the control of the mind. You can manipulate objects, animals, and people to see what you want them to see. Then there is the Arcane magic. Some of the dark users have this and for that reason, we couldn't study this." She stopped and went to fix Xander another bowl of stew.

"I had the ability to create an environment based on the feelings or the aura around me. That's why the flowers were always blooming, and the trees were always sturdy." She said.

"Your family thinks that that's a weak magic?" Maxi asked

"Yeah, compared to the other magic around us. You were either an Elemental, Mental, or an Arcane all the way. We were a piece of something, not whole."

"What is Lil Bit?" Josh asked. We all paid closer attention to this answer.

My mother smiled and shook her head. "My little Patience is all three."

"Fuck," Nick said angrily.

"Nesida also had all three, but she didn't use Arcane too much. She stuck with Elemental and Mental. But, when they killed Jackson, she let her Arcane magic take over. Arcane magic uses up your life energy every time it is used. So, when she killed the people that were threatening Patience, it took all the energy she had to use the magic she never wanted. She didn't use a buffer to balance it."

"Wait, so how is this any different from what we saw in Lil Bit." Dom asked.

"Unlike Nesida, Chaos feeds off Patience's wolf. That is unlimited energy and stamina that she can use to do whatever she wants." My mother said looking at everyone around the table. We all were worried at this point.

"Is there any way for me to help Queen, Ma?" I finally asked, ready for this conversation to be over with.

"You can try, sweetheart. When she turns into her darker being, ask her to call on her wolf. I don't know how well she is connected with her wolf, but it should overpower her." My mom replied.

"Shit, that's what happened to you in the office when Queen's Aunt Lurita vanished with her." Xavion added.

"That's right. Your Alpha ancestry don't like to share the body with no one. Not even magic that can enhance your wolf's power. It makes your wolf feel weak." My mother looked at me for more questions. I didn't have any to give her at the time. Right now, I felt that I needed to get back to Patience. Chaos was making an appearance every time Patience got angry.

"I know that you are mad at me for not telling you Xavier. I just wanted you to be stronger and capable of the things your father wasn't. When he came home, I felt the power of the Guardian around him. Someone put a spell on your father that night at the meeting. If he had the power that you have now, they wouldn't have gotten away with murdering Jackson and Nesida." My mother said to me sadly.

I knew losing my father the way she did was killing her inside. Whoever fucked with his brain had damaged some shit in his head. He started hallucinating and talking about a war that was going to happen with me leading it. We didn't know what to do with him. "It's ok, Mom. You don't have to worry about that anymore. Right now, I have to figure out how to keep Chaos from taking over Queen's body." I said out of frustration.

"We are here for you, bruh. You don't have to do this sh-stuff by yourself. Anything you need us to do, let us know and we got your back." Xander said.

"And you already know you got us." Nick said.

I dropped my head and thought of what I can do as her Alpha to keep my Queen from turning evil.

FIVE

Patience

---

*A*fter Xavier walked out, I took a shower and went downstairs to fix me some breakfast. To my surprise, breakfast was already cooked, and a plate of food was waiting for me at the breakfast bar. Even when he was mad at me, he still took the time to make sure that I was taken care of. I grabbed the plate and placed it in the microwave. When I turned around, Elder Nico was sitting at the table.

"Holy shit, you scared the fuck out of me. Where did you come from?" I asked as I grabbed my chest to steady my heartbeat. I was never caught off guard like that. I guess I was distracted by all this shit going on.

"I have been here. What are your plans for today." He answered nonchalantly.

"Umm, why are you here, Elder Nico." I asked him again, while ignoring his questions.

"I am here to protect you, Queen." He said devoid of any emotions.

"O-K, well I don't need to be protected. You can go and do shit that Elders do on a Wednesday morning."

"You can call me Nico, and I am not going anywhere. I am your guard."

I was about to go in on his ass, when the girls walked in the front door. "What's up bitch?" I heard Tori yell out.

"I am in the kitchen," I yelled back.

"No gurl, that's Queen Bitch." Loreen screamed after she walked into the kitchen. They all stared at Nico like he was here for another reason. "Well damn, P."

"Don't even think about it." I told Loreen. She was always looking for some scandal shit to talk about.

Nico looked at them and shook his head. "I will be in the study if you need anything. Do not leave this house, Queen." He told me in a fatherly tone. I didn't feel like addressing his ass, so I walked over to greet the girls. Jess was about to marry Xander in a couple of days and we were ready for the turn-up.

"Hey hoes, I thought y'all was going back to Texas this morning." I asked them.

"Nah bitch, I am staying until the wedding is over. Hopefully, I can find me one of them country ass men at the bachelor party." Tori said while smacking on her gum.

Jess looked over at her with confusion. "You do know that the bachelor party is for men, right."

"I know, I will be the only woman there, with a room full of niggas. Bitch, I got my outfit ready and a hotel room booked for that day." Tori replies. We all laughed at her dumb ass. She was always ready to jump on something, with her hot ass.

I walked us back into the family room and sat down, so that we can finish talking. Jess looked over at me and I knew what she wanted to do. She wanted to tell the girls about who I really was and what was going to happen at the mating ceremony. Ya see, Xander had to shift into his wolf and bite Jess on her shoulder during the reception. She already told her mom, and she was ok with that for some reason. I just didn't think that everybody was ready for the sounds that they will be making in the woods. I had a hard time with trying to block out my brothers having sex with their mates. I didn't want to hear Jess and Xander fucking.

I nodded my head at Jess for her to start talking. She shook her head and motioned for me to start. Loreen was looking at us and spoke on our behavior. "Look, if somebody got something to say, say that shit. What the fuck y'all holding back?" Tori picked her head up from her phone and checked us out.

"Bitches, I know y'all not holding secrets again." She said getting mad. I dropped my head back to get ready for whatever these hoes' reaction was going to be. 'Look," I started off. "I found out a lot of shit about myself these past few weeks. I found out that I am a Guardian, which y'all may call a witch. And I also can shift into a wolf." I ran through that shit. Tori and Loreen's faces were all bunched up in confusion. I didn't know if they didn't hear me or if they were processing the shit.

"Hold up. Hold up. You mean to tell me, that yo ass is an extra fa *Twilight*." Loreen said. You see that's why you can't tell these hoes nothing. She makes me sick. I rolled my eyes and continued talking to them.

"My father was an Alpha wolf over our clan, which is called the Satiniah pack."

"Holy shit, y'all worship Satan." Tori interrupted.

I ignored her stupid ass and continued again.

"My father and mother were murdered because the Guardians and the board of Alphas didn't approve. I found out that my Aunt Lurita was the queen of dark magic. And some of our memories have been erased due to some of our unexplainable events. Xavier is my mate and he is also the Alpha of his pack, along with Dom being the Alpha of our pack."

They looked at me with a lot of questions swarming in their heads. Loreen turned towards Jess and asked her a question. "And what yo bald head ass have to tell us?" Jess looked like she was about to back down, but the look on Tori's face made her think otherwise. She cleared her throat and started talking.

"Well, y'all know that Xander is a wolf because his brother is Xavier. I... I will have to leave right after the wedding to finish off the mating ceremony. We...Uhm...we have to go into the woods, so that he can shift while we make love. And...uhm. He has to bite me." Jess tried to explain. Loreen jumped up and you could see that she was not feeling this shit.

"Time the fuck out! What type of sacrificial lamb type of bullshit is going on." Loreen said.

"Look y'all," I tried to help Jess out, but Tori jumped in and stopped that.

"Nobody talking to you Bingo." She yelled at me. I was far from offended. I was shocked as shit that, that's what she called me. We were all trying not to laugh. I couldn't help but ask.

"Bitch, did you just call me a dog." She looked at me and we burst out laughing. These were my girls fa real. I was able to rely on them to pick me up and carry me through whatever.

"Bitch, y'all got me crying in here." Jess said still laughing at Tori's comment. We all sobered up and got real for a second.

"Why did y'all wait so long to tell us?" Tori said sounding wounded.

"I didn't know who or what I was. I am still figuring shit out. I just want y'all to be prepared for anything because I am pretty sure that it will be a lot of howling at the wedding." I told them. I knew that Tori and Loreen were feeling some type of way. I just didn't want them to overreact the way they usually do on things that they don't understand.

"Jess, are you ready for that? I mean, are you going to change into a wolf after the bite." Loreen asked.

"Yes, I am. I mean, in the beginning, I had my doubts because y'all know I was bouncing from man to man like y'all. But, with Xander, it's different. I am so in love with the security and passion he has for me. It is so unreal. He makes me feel like I am the center of his world." Jess said with a big smile on her face. I knew that my girl was happy. I just wished that my life was as simple as hers.

"So, Patience, you got a wand or something. How yo shit work." Tori asked with a little too much sass.

"What is your problem, like fa real. We told you, now stop being a bitch." I told her.

"No bitch, I'm mad. You know how much shit we could have

got away with if you had control over that shit earlier. No studying. No small dick men. No nothing." She said, smirking.

We all started laughing again. I knew that we would have been fucking shit up. Tori jumped up and start yelling. "Show me hoe. I need to see what you can do." These bitches were worse than kindergarteners. I didn't feel like doing shit, due to my dark side. I shook my head and told them no.

"No chicks. I am not about to put on some type of magic show, fa you hoes." I told them while walking to the kitchen. They followed and argued with me all the way there. Jess' stupid ass was ranting too like she has never seen me do anything. I frowned at them all. "I ain't doing shit. Get the fuck out my face."

They kept screaming for me to do something. Nico walked in to see what the hell was going on. He looked like he was ready to shift and chew my girls out. I chanted a spell under my breath and then it was silent. Tori looked around with the girls. You can see that Loreen was yelling for everyone outside to hear, but nothing was coming out. Nico smiled and nodded his approval, then went back into the office. I walked past them with a smile. Jess was trying to get my attention, but I ignored her. I sat, grabbed the remote, and turned on the TV. Tori jumped in front of it like, "Really bitch."

"No more show and tell shit, ok." I told her. She stumped her feet with all attitude but nodded her head. I gave them their voice back and they all started yelling at me again.

"Bitch, that was some tight shit." Loreen said. She started jumping up and down like a big ass kid. She was about to ask me to do something else.

"You won't get your voice back next time." I interrupted her. She closed her mouth and sat down with the rest of the girls.

"Jess, will you be a wolf after Xander bite you." Tori asked her again.

"No, I will have superhuman strength and I will age slower." She told them.

"No more Oil of Olay fa you bihh." Loreen said.

"Y'all are too stupid." I said smiling.

Jess and I answered all of their stupid questions. I didn't mind it, though. It was better than sitting here and being upset with Xavier. Now that my friends knew what was going on, I had to really get my darker side under control. Tori was talking about ticks and fleas, when Xavier walked in. Tori and Loreen stopped to stare at him in the new light that I put him in. Xavier was looking unsure for a minute and then turned towards me for answers. I knew something crazy was about to come out of that hoe mouth, when Tori cleared her throat.

"So, Xavier, do you have a collar for that bitch neck, or what?" Tori asked. Xavier started laughing his ass off. I didn't find that shit funny at all, but the way that he was laughing, made me smile.

"Nah, I got that crown for her head, though." He said while staring into my eyes.

"Well, on that note, we out of here. We'll see you later, boo." Jess said, getting up and heading to the door with the girls. The girls said their goodbyes without any other comments and left me alone with my Alpha. He was still staring at me and it had me uneasy. Xavier started walking to me with his hands in his pockets. He was dressed in some jeans and a red t-shirt. He made the simplest shit look so good. He kneeled in front of me and grabbed my hand.

"I am sorry for how I walked out on you. It was disrespectful, and it won't happen again." He said to me while kissing on my hand. He looked up into my eyes and continued talking. "How do you feel, Queen?" The way he asked that had me ready to jump on him. It was soft and sexy in his deep strong voice. My hands were still in his and I knew that he was able to see in my eyes where I was ready to go from there.

He smiled and pulled his bottom lip in between his teeth. "Maybe I should get you a collar Queen, cuz I can see that you are about to be very bad."

"I thought you liked it that way." I teased.

He opened my legs to place his body in between them. I could feel my eyes changing into my wolf and the ache in my gums. Xavier's eyes changed with mine. "Queen," he warned. I took a deep breath to bring my Alpha side back in. I couldn't help it. Every time my wolf felt another unrelated Alpha in the room, she showed herself. I was being controlled by a dark bitch, who wants out of my body, and a territorial wolf. I couldn't win for losing.

I sat back and let out a sigh. I just wanted my body and mind back. Xavier was always in my head, along with Dom. I didn't have any privacy with Nico hanging around. Xavier was staring at me and trying to get in my head. I looked at him and shut him out. His frown let me know how unhappy he was with that.

"Open the fuck up, Queen."

I pushed him back and got up. "Can you please stay out of my head for just a minute?" I yelled getting frustrated.

"I wouldn't have to do that Queen if you talk to me." He said, calmly.

"I would, if you give me a chance to." I sighed. "I just feel like a lot of shit is going on and I don't know how to figure this shit out."

"You don't have to figure this shit out on your own Queen. My mom told me some things that may help us figure things out." He got up, walked towards me, and pulled me into his strong arms. "We can't figure this shit out if you shut down on me." He whispered to me. We stayed this way for a while, until Nico walked in and told Xavier to answer his phone that we have been ignoring for the past fifteen minutes.

"Please answer your got damn phone." He said and walked back into the office.

"Do he stay here now?" I asked Xavier.

"He is here to protect you Queen, when I'm not here." He said, while reaching for his phone. "What's up?" He asked. You can see that his mood went from my Alpha to the pack's Alpha. "I'll be right there." He said and hung up. "I gotta go. We will talk more, and I will finish off what you started when I get back." He said before kissing me into agreeing with anything that came out of his mouth.

"I love you. Don't leave the house without Nico." He said, giving me a short soft kiss and leaving the house. I was going to go see my brothers, but I wanted things to cool down some more. I went into the office to see what Nico was doing. I opened the door and to my surprise, he was sitting in the chair facing the door.

"Uhm, what are you doing in here?" I asked him.

"I wanted some quiet time, but the way the women were in there with all that noise, Xavier's phone, and your confused mind, it became difficult." He explained.

"How do you know what I am thinking?" I said, walking into the room and taking the seat behind the desk. He swiveled the chair to face me. His eyes were burning into mine, and it felt uncomfortable. "You don't know how much magic you have built up inside." He told me.

"You're right," I said as I clasped my hand together on the desk. "But, I guess you do. Why don't you do me a favor and tell me about it."

"Not my place, Queen." He answered. He got up and was about to walk out the door.

"Wait," I stopped him. He turned and waited for me to continue. "Is there something that you need to tell me or something that I need to know." I asked him. He smiled and ignored my question completely.

"I will cook you something to eat and then we will have that silence." He told me and walked out the office. I sat back and let out a sigh. I was so tired of all the cryptic messages. Everyone knew some secret about me and that shit was getting aggravating.

I made some calls to Jess and my brothers to check on some things. I ate the lunch that Nico prepared and then we went for a run with a couple more wolves from the pack. I learned some things about the history of Xavier's pack and it wasn't any different from my own. Jess called me and asked me about some dress that she wanted us to wear. So, I was in the office, on the computer for the remainder of the day. By the time I was done, the sun had set, and I was tired. I didn't hear Xavier come in, and that had me worried, until Nico told me that he came in an hour ago.

"He heard you ranting with your friend about some stupid ass dress and decided not to bother you." He said nonchalantly.

"O-k, you can leave, now that my Alpha is home." I told him. He gave me that stupid ass smile again and got up to leave.

"Goodnight, Queen." I went upstairs to see Xavier. When I opened the door, he was in the bed knocked out. He looked so tired.

He has been busy the past few days. I went to take a shower and jumped in the bed with my Alpha. He wrapped his arms around me and sleep took over in no time.

～

I walked towards the front door where there are eight guards.

"State your business here." One of them stated.

I took in a deep breath and released it out into the air. "My business is to kill every Guardian in this facility." I said in a voice that I didn't recognize. It was sharp and hollow.

"Sound the alarm." The other stated. I gave them the time to call in their reinforcements. Men and women came out in their cloaks. But, the one that I was looking for wasn't present. The one that sent those assassins to kill my parents. An older man walked out dressed like the dude off of Demolition Man, with a white long cone hat, dressed in all white. I smiled and greeted him as he stepped forward.

"Greetings," I said, sarcastically, while waving my hand in a circular motion.

"State your business or leave this facility." He said.

"Hmm…Why ask questions, when all you will give me is lies? I rather skip that part and save myself the time that you'll waste." I told him.

"If you do not state your business, we will have to act hostile." He responded.

"Well, I guess you gotta do what you have to do, but please allow me to act first." I said in a deeper voice. I can feel his magic building, along with the rest of them around him. I didn't have to charge up. I been ready since I was six. I waved my hand and the older man dropped. He became dull, and his eyes became a pale grey. I inhaled the air, which his energy released in. "Hmm," I moaned out my satisfaction. The others around him were stunned. I knew that my power surpassed everyone here in this facility, and this is their first-time witnessing greatness.

"Bu-but, she didn't chant a spell." The guard said trembling.

"Oh, how I forget sometimes of the weaker ones. Let me make this easier for you."

"For the fire that burns inside of me

I unlock that chain to set you free
For those who are present, is the ones to blame
Set the bodies up into flame"
I stood and watched as every guard around the facility, was set on fire. They tried the drop and roll method, but that human shit wouldn't put out this fire. *Nothing will.* I walked through the flames and into the facility, where there were other guards lined up.

"Good, more playmates that want to play with me."

Chaos

I woke up ready to finish what I started. I got a lot of information from the Guardians Southern Facility. I tried to get up but was trapped by something. I didn't feel threatened in any kind of way. I turned towards this powerful energy that was leaking out of this man's pores. I am not surprised when I see the beautiful man that is always there when I awake. I placed my hand on his face and by pure instinct, he grabbed and kissed it.

Goddamn.

He let my hand go, and kissed me softly on my lips, with his eyes still closed. I again caressed his face. My hands traveled down to his neck, and then to his chest. His breathing picked up and a slight groan came from his now parted lips. I couldn't believe that I had complete control over this man, without using magic but the feelings were mutual.

My body was reacting the same way. It was throbbing to be touched, grabbed, or bitten by this man. I grabbed his hand and placed it under my shirt. His warm skin against my cool body had me in overdrive. *Shit.* What type of magic did he have over my body? I felt weak, like I gave him this control.

"Your body is freezing, Queen. Let me warm you up." He whispered.

I didn't know what Patience did with him when he acted this way. But, I was about to shut this shit down. I pulled the covers back and looked at the magnificent piece that was hanging off his leg. I licked my lips and felt the growl in my throat. *Not this time little wolf,* I told her and pushed her back in. I crawled and got in between his legs. He placed his hands behind his head like this shit was going to be a breeze. *Nah wolfie. You betta hold on.*

I placed my hand on his leg and kissed up his hard body. He tried to open his eyes, but I kept them close with a little magic. He didn't complain. He sat back and relaxed. I kissed his lips and headed back down his body. He was moaning out her name, like she was present. I was thinking of letting myself be known, so that I can get the credit. But I was going to let him figure it out on his own. His golden rod was hard and ready to enter wherever I wanted it to. I kissed the tip of his dick. It was a taste that only could be described as him. His wolf was ready to take control as well, but I was not done. I needed more. That small taste wasn't enough to quench my thirst. I took him all the way in my mouth this time and swallowed him whole.

"Fuck, Queen." He growled out, and I was loving it. I pulled his hip up towards my face. The kisses were still being sent up and down his body with some more of my magic. This beautiful man was all mine to handle. He removed his hands from behind his head and grabbed my head. "Queen slow down, fuck." He demanded. The control he thought that he was going to have, was slipping.

I ignored him. I was thirsty, and I planned on milking him dry. I placed my hand on his chest so that I can intensify all his sensitive areas. He began to get wild and his wolf started coming out. I sucked harder and his release was nothing that I couldn't handle. I swallowed every drop of his little wolf babies.

"Oh shit, baby. What the fuck was that?" He asked.

"You taste so good, beautiful one. Please tell me that you have a lot more to give." I told him.

He jumped up and looked into my eyes. "Are you fucking serious? Where is my fucking Queen?"

"She's sleeping right now. Please, let's not wake her up. I'm pretty sure that you can find other things to do with this body." I told him, now turning my back towards him. I bent over with my chest on the bed and my legs spread wide. He shook his head and got out of the bed. He was mumbling to his self about what we did wasn't right. I didn't know what he was talking about. He was going to finish whether he liked it or not. I turned around and faced him. "Come on my Beautiful One, give me what I need freely, or I can take it." I told him. He turned around with fury in his eyes. Good, I liked it rough. "You can't make me do shit. Bring my fucking Queen back." He growled.

I wasn't scared at all. He would never harm his Queen. "I am in charge of this body at this moment. Your Queen isn't strong enough to hold me back. Maybe you should think of ways to get on my good side, before you get all wolfie on me." I said. I stood and turned my back towards him. I bent down with my ass up. "Come get on my good side; it's better than my bad side, trust me." I told him. Xavier was staring at my pussy like a hungry animal. He licked his lips and walked forward. I wasn't prepared for what was next. He pushed my body down and his teeth locked onto my swollen nub.

"Hmm," I moaned out. It felt so good. He started sucking and licking. He spread my cheeks and licked me from my nub all the way up to my lower back. He nipped both of my ass cheeks and stood behind me. He caressed my ass before smacking the shit out of me. I didn't flinch. I had enough back there for him to do whatever he wanted. I shook my ass for him and that was his undoing.

Xavier snatched my waist and made sure I stayed in position. He didn't have to worry, though. My body needed this. "Keep in mind beautiful one, I am not your sweet Queen. I can handle your wolf." I told him. And with no further instruction, he pushed so deep inside of me, that I thought I felt him in my stomach. "Fuck." I yelled out.

"You can't take shit." He taunted.

His nails were digging into my skin and I could feel my blood dripping from the wounds. He went in and out with long deep strokes. I didn't feel that he wanted me like he did in the beginning. I guess that was the love he was feeling for Patience before he found out that it was me. That was fine as well. As long as he cured the ache between my legs, he could feel however the fuck he wanted. I tried to move to his rhythm, but he slapped me on my ass and pulled my head back by my dark hair.

"Don't fucking move." He growled harshly in my ear. I can feel his canines nipping at my earlobe. His strokes became harsher and harder. My mind was everywhere, but where it needed to be. The feelings that were building up inside me was new and unexpected. I moaned and concentrated on staying awake for this ending. There was no way that his Queen was getting the end result of this. I'll let her suffer through the aftermath. I felt my walls tightening around his rod. The pressure to let go of the tension, the vengeance, and everything that I had my mind set on, was dissolving because of this good of how he was making me feel. I screamed out my release and fell forward. If this was what his Queen was getting on a daily, I was coming back every night for it.

SIX

Xavier
---

*T*he next morning was uncomfortable. I got up, took a shower, and started breakfast. I knew that Nico was probably on his way to the house. I wanted to have a conversation with Queen before he got here to see what she remembered. I was fixing up her plate, when I felt her coming near. I turned towards the kitchen door, as she approached it.

"Good morning," I said, while watching her walk in.

"Hey baby, you cook me breakfast, again." She asked sweetly. She went to the table and winced before sitting.

"What's wrong, Queen?" I asked, knowing the answer already.

"I don't know. My body is aching for some reason. I used to sleepwalk a lot at home, without Aunt Lurita knowing. I guess I ran into something hard and sharp. I can see that I was cut, but it is healing." She said and raised up her shirt to show me the bruises that I put on her last night. I brought her breakfast to the table and kneeled to check on her wounds. Her skin was purple in the area, but it looked like it was healing faster than it should. I leaned in and kissed them softly, then apologized for them.

"I'm sorry, Queen." I told her sadly. I never wanted to hurt her.

"It's ok, my Alpha. Sleepwalking is not something I need

protecting from." She said, while rubbing her hands through my dreads. "It looks like you need a touch-up. Would you like to sit between these legs?" She whispered teasingly.

"I would love your hands stroking my head." I told her, caressing her with my hands still underneath her shirt. I had to calm myself down knowing that her body needed to fully heal before we could do anything. I kissed her softly and pulled back. "Eat Queen. Food will help you heal quicker."

She looked up at me confused. She wanted to say something, but the look in my eyes told her don't.

"I wanted to tell you what I found out yesterday at my mother's house." I went back to grab my two plates of food. "My mother told me that she was a Mental Guardian. Her family doesn't have all the magic of them, just a piece. That made them not so popular in the Guardian world. When they found out that she transferred her power to me, they tried to take me from her, but my dad threatened to kill them. She also said that your mother went to see them before she was murdered. I will be going up there to find out what happened with that conversation with Nick." I told her.

"I'm coming with you." She interrupted.

"No, you're not. If you had better control over your magic Queen, I'll take you. But, we need to gather some information from them and I can't do that if I am worried about you." I said, looking into her eyes. I thought that she was going to fight me on it, but surprisingly she doesn't.

"My mother told me about your magic. That you have the Mental, Elemental, and Arcane magic." I continued.

"Are you fucking serious? I have a piece of all of three?" She asked.

"No, Queen. Not just a piece. You are all three." I told her. She was shocked, and that shit confused me. I thought that her Aunt Lurita was working with her. Why the fuck didn't she tell her about all the magic she possessed? Why focus on one? Nico walked in without knocking.

"Morning," he said barely over a whisper.

"Nico, knock before you come into my home, with my Queen."

I told him straight up. He nodded his understanding and walked over to the coffee pot. I got up and placed my dishes in the sink. "I am going to the station. If you need me or anything while I'm out, call me. You understand." I told her. She got up, walked towards me, and wrapped her arms around my neck.

"Yes, Alpha."

I picked up my keys and was heading towards the door. "Whenever you're ready to hear my story, let me know. Queen looks like she is well enough, don't you think." The asshole said to me when I got to the door. I turned around and faced them both. He was sipping on his coffee like he didn't just say that shit. "Why wait until I get to the door to say something?" I asked.

"I didn't think about it until now. Do you want to know or not?" He told me not casually.

I let out a sigh and began to walk back to the table where Queen was sitting. She looked confused about the conversation. I leaned over and told her what was going on. "Nico is about to tell us why he is here all the goddamn time."

She dropped her fork and gave her full attention. "Please do tell."

Nico walked over to the table with his coffee in hand. He sat and took in a couple of breaths. I looked over at an impatient Queen. She started drumming her hand on the table to get him to start talking. I don't know if he was waiting for her to calm down or what. But, I had better things to do than to sit and watch his ass breathe in and out.

"When your mother came over to the southern territory to replace our last Guardian, we were relieved. She took her time to speak to us, and all the other Elders before taking the job. Nesida showed great interest and promised us better days. She started performing her duties as soon as she recited the pledge. She worked with all our problems and didn't turn no one away. When she came to Destrehan, Felix was the first one she met up with. He flirted and tried his hardest to get with your mom, but she shut him down.

Jackson was the next one that she had to meet. Everyone thought that your father went rogue. So, Jacob and I accompanied her to his home. Your brothers were there alone with your father roaming the woods. Nesida did her feel of the earth thing, and we found Jack where his first mate was killed. He started growling as we approached. Nesida told me and Jacob to stay back. We disagreed, until she started glowing. She approached your father with love surrounding her. That was what your father needed at the time. He looked up at her and saw the light for the first time. That was the day we got our friend back.

I was in the room with the other Elders discussing some territorial issues. I was the last one to leave the office, when the Guardians Assassins came for me. I was far from scared, but I knew that this was a losing battle. Nesida came out of nowhere and saved me before they could lay a hand on me. I vowed to protect her for the rest of her life.

Your Alpha can tell you that when an Elder gives you his word, it is a bond that is made that can never be broken. When the assassins came for you and your parents, your mother told me to protect you. That was going to be me making it up to her. But, she didn't know that Aunt Lurita came to see me. She made her threats about protecting her sister and her family. She made frequent visits about that and other things. But, I lost you when they put me on some kind of spell to sleep. When I woke up you were gone, and your parents were deceased." He told us. I hope he didn't think that he was fooling anybody with the frequent visit shit. The way he was looking at her when she walked in, said everything that didn't need to be said.

"So, you are protecting me because my mother saved you." Queen asked.

"Yes Queen. I am also your other Godfather."

"Man, get the fuck out of here. You not fucking around,right?" I said in surprise.

Queen was looking with her mouth dropped open. She didn't understand what this meant but I did. And it was smart on Nesida's part. All the Elders had to agree to any subject. If one disagreed, it was never going to be settled until they all agreed. If Nico was on the board of Elders, and the subject of me and Queen came up, he was there to disagree. I smiled at that thought. Nesida knew that we were going to be together no matter what came our way. I just hoped that I was making her proud right now.

"Now, that you got my story, you can stop asking me bullshit questions." He said. He got up and walked into the office without another word. Queen was still silent about the whole thing. I grabbed her hand and squeezed it a little.

"Are you good?" I asked her.

"Yeah. It's just a lot to take in right now. I'll be ok, though. Go to work and do your Alpha duties." She gets up and placed them plump lips on me. "I love you, Alpha. Come home safe."

I left the house and went to the station. Things have been quieter since Chaos got rid of Felix and his family. Insignificant calls have been coming in and they didn't need my attention as much. I wanted to talk to my brothers about what happened last night with Chaos.

I gave everyone their orders and asked my brothers to meet me in my office. When we were all settled in, I told them what happened. Xander was already shaking his head at my actions, but Xavion looked at it a different way.

"What if you could manipulate her?" He asked.

"What the fuck do you mean by that? This is our Queen, dumb ass." Xander disagreed with Xavion.

"If X can get control of her this way, why not. At least she would be in plain sight and not drowning people in a ball of water and shit. She already showed us how much she doesn't like being controlled. What if during sex X exercises control there? Control her pleasure, see what that will do."

"I don't know about that Xavion. That's like playing with fire." I told him.

"It's worth the try." He replied, and then continued. "Try talking to her, find out her weakness and exploit it."

I sat back in my seat and sighed. I really didn't want to do this, but I had to do something. I switched the subject up and talked about Xander's mating ceremony. "Are you ready for the ceremony?" I asked him.

He shook his head again tiredly this time. "Man, I just can't wait for this shit to be over with. She got bridesmaids with dresses and shit. I tried to tell her that we don't do all that, but she wasn't having it. She told me that everything was different for her." He said.

"She is going to be your mate, Xander. You gotta do whatever makes her happy." Xavion told him.

"Oh yeah, you guys gotta go get fitted for the tux that you guys have to wear." Xander told us.

"Hell nah. I ain't wearing that shit. What the fuck we look like. The ceremony is in the fucking front yard of mom's house. Full of dirt." Xavion ranted.

"Whatever happened to make your mate happy?" Xander replied with a smirk.

"That's your mate, bruh. I ain't wearing that shit." Xavion said much slower than last time. He wanted Xander to know that he wasn't fucking around.

"Andy, see if Jessica could compromise a little. We can do linen." I told him.

"Yeah, I can fuck with that." Xavion agreed.

"Cool, I'll suggest it, but it can go easier if you tell Queen to suggest it. Jess already think that we don't know shit. She called us country boys and shit." Xander replied.

"I'll run it by her. I got to go by Nick's and discuss when we will be leaving to go see our Mom's people." I told them. We split up and went our separate ways for the day. I hope what we discuss earlier works because I was out of options at this point.

SEVEN

Matteo

I was standing in the woods, near the Guardian's Southern Facility. They had a lot of the Guardians surrounding the area, along with their trackers and the board members. There were body bags and other bodies spread out all over the ground. Some of them were mutilated more than others. Somebody fucked this place up.

There was dark magic all around this place. It was mature and heavy. This was the same magic that woke me up out of my sleep the other day. I felt it every time that it was awakened. It felt familiar, but stronger than anything that I have ever witnessed. Whoever done this shit was going to have a lot of heat on them. Fuck, I'll join his team. I knew that one of these muthafuckers had something to do with my daughters being killed. I was looking at the scene before me, when I felt the movement behind me. I didn't flinch. I recognized them scary bitches anywhere.

"I don't think that you belong here, friend. Unless you are looking for trouble." This leeching fuck said. When you use dark magic without buffers, you began to age, rot, and develop a deadly odor. An odor that only can be described as death itself. Dumb assholes that didn't know how to use magic became this.

That was another reason why I joined the Guardian facility. I learned what I could, to use the magic that I had. Hope didn't know that I was taking energy from her to succeed in this. The Mental magic worked best with Arcane magic. I am the master of both. I dib and dab a little with Elemental, but learning to mind fuck someone brought joy to my dark soul.

One of the things that was with Bacchus cleared its throat to get my attention. There were four of them. These bitches deserved my back. But, he was bold enough to step closer to me. "Did you just ignore Lord Bacchus, you fucking prick? Turn around and bow to him." His dumb ass had the audacity to say to me. That was the type of insolence that had me ready to level the world and shit. How muthafuckers just be putting Lord in front their name like they earned the right to.

"I don't recall you being a Lord when I went in, Bacchus. I'm pretty sure you ain't one now. So, do you and your garbage ass band, crew, or whatever y'all calling each other a favor, and get the fuck out of my face." I told them, with my back still turned. I was still watching the Guardians gather residue from each of the piles of ashes that was spread across the land.

"Who the fuck do- "

"I am the Lord of Darkness, mutha fucker. I think that you need to shut the fuck up and bow down to me." I turned and showed off my black eyes. They all dropped down to their knees with no hesitation. I didn't want to draw any attention to myself, but I had to discipline at least one, to show them that I was back. I chanted for a painful but silent death for the one who approached me. He screamed out with no sound. Blood was leaking out from everywhere. The others knew not to pick their fucking head up to see shit. I walked up to Bacchus, as his friend reached out for help. They all yanked their arms away from him and let their boy suffer. "Nah, you know that this little stunt is going to cost you."

"Sorry, my Lord. We didn't know that it was you. We thought that they killed you in the prison. That was what the Supremes has been telling everyone." Bacchus told me. This was probably what had the Guardians doing fucked up assassin shit. I needed to get the information from the person that tore this bitch up. I'm pretty sure that they didn't leave empty-handed.

"I am only going to ask once. Who did this?" I asked.

"Some dark bitch." Bacchus replied quickly. "She used magic without chanting. After she took out the guards, she began going through the facility, tearing them up with long black claws. She bit a man's face off and spat it out into another Guardian's face. But, what was crazy, was that she took in all of their powers without blowing up. When she turned towards the woods, where we were watching, her face was of a wolf, with red eyes. It didn't look like one of those crazy rouge wolves up north. She had complete control over it."

"How do you know that she controlled this wolf?" I asked. The information that he gave me, I already knew who it was. I was happy to know that my baby girl was getting a head start on things. But, her going rouge was not going to help the situation. I had to put a lot of those crazy bitches down. If this was the route that she was going, I was going to have to live with that. Because no one was going to take my last living descendant from me.

"My Lord, she changed back into the woman in front of my eyes and winked. She knew that we were there and didn't attack us. But, she did send us a warning to not come near the facility until she was finished with it herself. We came by to see if there was any energy left to consume." Bacchus answered.

Holy shit. That means her dark magic learned to be one with her rouge wolf. If my little Patience didn't learn how to do what her dark side has done, she will be overpowered. I didn't know how to train her to be good, but I did know how to train her to be one with her dark side.

"We know who done this. We will have to meet up with the other Supremes and the other council members. Tell them that we will need everyone involved to kill the half-breed." One of the Guardians said, after examining all the evidence they needed to attack my granddaughter. These muthafuckers just didn't know.

"Thank you, Bacchus. But your insolence cannot be forgiven. I don't think that death will cure you of being stupid. Let's just hope that where you are going, you are surrounded by dumb mutha-fuckers just like you." I told him and gave them all the same death as I did with their friend.

EIGHT

Xavier
_____

I had to deal with a lot of petty shit today. Xavion been hinting that he wanted to get with Loreen but didn't want to ask her to be his date for the wedding. He didn't want to give her any ideas of them mating. The way Loreen acted I didn't think that was going to be a problem. I told Xavion that he was going to be the one to get hooked. Queen talked to Jessica about the linen outfits that we could wear to the wedding.

We tried them on in front of the girls except for Jessica. The girls were drooling but Queen was like fuck no. I didn't see what the problem was until she pointed to my third leg. I didn't know what she wanted us to do about that. It was natural.

"Queen, you can't see it that much." I told her. All of her friends burst out laughing.

"Yeah right fool, we can see it. I'm pretty sure that all of the women that will be attending the ceremony will see it, too. Y'all need to pick something else to wear, before your Queen zap them hoes." Tori said, still laughing.

"I don't see nothing wrong with it. Do you, Loreen?" That fool Xavion said flirting.

"Naw, I don't. You are not mine, so I can't be mad at you for wearing that. P has every right to be." She answered. Xavion didn't like the answer at all. I thought I heard him growling, but as many times as he saw her, he would have been claimed her as his. Something was off about the whole situation.

Queen got up and stood in front of me. "You don't see anything wrong with what you are wearing?" She asked. I shook my head no. We saw each other naked every time we shift. I wasn't ashamed of my shit. "Ok, then." She said casually. Her girls were shaking their heads knowingly. "While you guys are here, tell us what y'all think of our dresses." She continued. The girls jumped up and laughed all the way to the back of the store.

I was cool with that. We got dressed in our regular clothes and waited for the girls to come out in their dresses. Loreen and Tori came out in a tight, fitted dress. The shit was short and had a deep v in front of the dress. Xander was shaking his head with laughter, while Xavion was shaking his head with a scowl on his face. This fool was big mad for real. I couldn't clown him like I wanted, because Queen came out with a dress so short that if she bent over, everyone was going to see my shit. I jumped up and knocked down the rack of clothes.

"Fuck no! You ain't wearing that shit. Go back in there and tell them to change them fucking dresses. Fuck that." I turned towards a laughing Xander. "Look bruh, tell Jess to change that shit. Queen is not, I repeat, is not walking nowhere in that fucking dress."

"So, I can't wear my dress, but you can wear your linen." She asked with her hand on her hip. I didn't know if it was the girls that was giving her this extra boost of confidence to question me. But I already told her that, that shit wasn't allowed. Her fucking mouth was going to get her fucked up in front of everybody. I walked up to her and she held her hand up. I took her hand and yanked her towards me. "Don't. Fucking, Play. With. Me." I demanded.

"I am not playing with you, Alpha. The same way that you are possessive of me, I am the same way with you. I don't want them women seeing you like that." She reached down and grabbed my shit possessively. "This. Is. Mine." She growled at me. Her hazel eyes were shining through. Her Alpha side was laying her law down and was waiting for me to deny her what was rightfully hers. My shit was getting harder in her hand. I kissed her lips and nipped it before pulling back.

"You got that, Queen. Yo Xander, see if they got something else that won't have my Queen going all Alpha on me." I told him with my eyes still on my Queen.

"Y'all are fucking crazy." Xander said. He got up and changed our outfit. It didn't change much. It was hard to hide what we were blessed with. We continued our day with Xavion flirting and throwing hints at Loreen. She didn't budge, though. She didn't want nothing to do with him. We sat and had lunch with the rest of the gang. I received a call from the station which pulled me away for the rest of the day.

When I got home, Queen was already sleeping. I was hoping to get her before she went to sleep. The way her body was calling for me, had me ready to bend her ass over in the dressing room. I took a shower and jumped in the bed. Queen had some silk cap on her head. The side of her face was sweating. I touched her body and it was cold. I knew my baby wasn't getting sick. I pulled her body, to face me. When she opened her eyes, they were a whiskey brown but was changing before my eyes. They went from green, yellow, black, and then went to a blood red.

"Hi my Beautiful One. Did you miss me?" Chaos said.

I got out of bed and was headed to the guest room. I didn't want to do this shit again. I felt like I was betraying my Queen. When I got to the door, it closed shut and locked on its own. "Open the door, Chaos." I told her. She laughed at me. I turned around to face her. She took the silk cap off her head. Her black hair fell around her face.

"Must we go through this every night." She said to me. "You must not want to see your Queen again." She threatened. I didn't know how much damage she can do to Queen, but I didn't want to test it.

I closed my eyes and shut completely down. I didn't want her to feel loved, liked, or cared for. If fucking her was all I had to do to keep her calm, then I could do that. But all this control she thought she had, was about to be taken. I didn't give a fuck how dark she was. I was her Alpha as well. And after tonight, she was going to remember that.

I opened my eyes, with no emotion in them. I stalked to the bed and snatched her ass off of it. I ripped her nightgown off and threw her down. She laughed and was enjoying herself. I pulled my pants down and grabbed my dick. Her laughing stopped, and she stared at me stroking my shit with hunger in her eyes. "Is this what you want?" I asked. She looked up at me and didn't answer. I continued stroking. Precum was leaking from the tip of my dick. She growled and leaned forward to take me in her mouth. "No," I told her and pulled back. "Do you want this?" I asked.

"I can tie you up and take what I want. I can make you do what I want you to do. Don't think that you are controlling shit here." She hissed out.

"But how better would it be if I did it willingly." I replied.

She started thinking of my reply. I was hoping that she went for it. I didn't want to think too much because I knew that she would have been able to read my mind. I continued stroking myself and she was becoming impatient. She bit her lip before answering the first question. "Yes, I want it." She growled.

"Are you sure?" I teased her.

"Yes," she snapped.

"On your knees." I told her.

She shook her head. "I want to taste you first."

"I didn't ask you want you wanted. Get. On. Your. Fucking. Knees. NOW!" I growled.

She smiled before turning around and getting on her knees. I walked behind her and placed the tip of my dick near her opening. I slid the tip in and pulled out. I slid a little more in and pulled out again. I teased her like that for a minute before she began to get wild. She tried to get up, but I pushed her back down. "Do you want this?" I repeated.

"I told you yes already." She moaned when I pushed inside her.

"Who am I?" I asked.

"What," she said confused.

"Who am I to you, Chaos?" I asked, this time going deeper with every stroke.

"I am not your Queen." She ignored.

I pulled all the way out and slapped her on the ass. "That's not what I fucking asked you." I told her with another slap. She moaned and placed her hand between her legs. I took her hand and placed it on the bed. "Don't touch or grab shit but them sheets. You do it again and we will start all over. Do you understand that?" I told her.

"Yes," she said without hesitation this time. I pushed her body down further. Her pussy was dripping wet. I slid my dick across her nub and she shivered.

"I will ask you one last time. Who am I to you" I asked now sliding the tip into her opening.

"My Alpha," she replied, finally. I wasn't satisfied with that.

"Who do you belong to?" I demanded. She took a deep breath before answering.

"You, my Alpha."

Gotcha. I pushed all the way inside her without holding back. I pulled her hair back, where she could look into my eyes. "That is how you will address me from now on. Do you understand?" I said while giving her those deep strokes.

"Yes, Alpha." She moaned out.

"Good." I told her and fucked her through the night.

NINE

Patience
_____

$\mathscr{I}$ had been waking up every morning for the past week sore as shit. I tried to stay up last night for as long as I could, but I have been even more tired than usual. X and I hadn't been talking like we used to. He would wake up in the morning with breakfast, and then he disappears for the whole day. He comes back tired and the shit is bothering me. I can't tell you that last time that we had sex or a kiss that made me weak in my knees. He has been giving me these dry ass kisses lately, and that shit had me wondering.

Was he cheating on me? I didn't want to go overboard and accuse my Alpha of anything. But, come on man, he hasn't touched me in a minute. I think that it was the bruises and the wounds that I was showing him. There was always proof of me getting into something. It looked like my body was recovering from bites on my leg. I asked X about it and he didn't inspect this one like he did the others.

Our conversations have been getting stranger as well. They would be clipped and straight to the point without all the extra details. I liked the details. It made our conversations last longer, and I loved to hear his voice. I was sitting in the family room waiting for him to come home. I called his office and left a message for him. For some reason, I haven't been able to communicate with him telepathically. I guess the distance between the two of us was putting a strain on that.

Nico came in after I left the message to see if there was a problem that he can solve. I told him that it was something that only my Alpha could cure. He told me that he was going to go running for a couple of hours and left quickly. We had got pretty close since he told us who he really was. I was happy to have a father figure in my life. He has been teaching me a lot of things about my wolf. I felt more connected with her. I have learned to control her when she tries to escape from me. Nico couldn't teach me anything about Chaos or my Guardian side, though.

Xavier came through the door, ready for whatever. I told Nico not to tell Xavier about what I needed. I wanted him to come right away without knowing why. He was always doing shit for the pack. I needed him to be my Alpha for the remainder of the day.

"What's wrong Queen?" He rushed over and grabbed me. He examined me and waited for my answer.

"I need you my Alpha. I have been needing you for a while now." I asked while caressing his face. He looked irritated at first. Like I was bothering him. I know you fucking lying. I dropped my hand and took a step back. "Look, if you don't want me, let me know. Because I can get the fuck, fa real."

His look didn't change. "This is what you called me home for. To bitch?"

"Tha fuck. What is going on with you? You never talked to me like this. Is it another bitch. Let me know. I can pack my shit and go home, nigga." I told him getting mad.

"It's not another woman, Queen." He sighed. "It is just a lot of shit going on right now, that I am trying to figure out with my brothers and Dom's pack. We are trying to make sure Xander and Jess' mating ceremony go as plan. I don't want no shit popping up on us at the last minute." He grabbed me and pulled me to him. "I'm sorry, baby."

Let me tell y'all something. When he called me his Queen, that shit made me want to sit on top of the world on a throne, with a crown on top of my head. But, when he called me baby in that Alpha voice and in the New Orleans accent, I be ready to spread my legs wide open for him. I licked my lips anticipating what I knew he was about to give me. He gives me that wolf smirk and his hold became tighter. "Tell me Queen, what do you need from your Alpha." He said with that sexy as drawl. I was wearing one of his shirts with nothing else. I needed him to have easy access to this pussy.

"As my Alpha, I thought you would know that already." I teased him.

He picked me up and I wrapped my legs around his waist. He put me on the nearest wall and began to rip my shirt off. Some of the bruises were still tender, but I couldn't let that get in the way with the ache in between my legs. "I can smell you, Queen."

"I taste better," I taunted.

"Let's see about that." He told me and went into the kitchen. He sat me on top of the island and spread my legs wide. Without warning, he dove in and attacked my pussy like he was starving. He was humming and groaning.

"Yes, Alpha, take all you need. Fuck!" I yelled.

He wasn't having no mercy on me. My Alpha's tongue felt like it was getting thicker and longer. He licked and sucked until I had not one but two orgasms back to back. He pulled back, dropped his pants, and pushed that pipe inside of me. "Fuck," I yelled.

He was going so hard on me. The shit felt good, but it was different. There was no passion or feeling in this. It felt more like fucking than anything. For the first time, I wasn't enjoying this at all. I would rather for him to put his tongue back on me. He wrapped his hand around my throat. "Do you like it like this Queen or, are you ready for me to bite you." He told me. His other hand was holding onto my legs. His nails started growing into my skin and he was becoming feral.

"X, stop," I told him while trying to remove his hand from around my neck.

"No, you called me for this dick. You going to take it, the way I give it to you." He growled out. His wolf eyes were showing, at least I think that they are. His eyes were turning black.

"Xavier, get off of me." I yelled. I started scratching and kicking, but he still didn't let go. I chanted for my shockwaves to hit my body, which hit his. He flew back and shifted into his wolf. His wolf didn't recognize me. It was growling and showing me his teeth. I raised my hand to try and talk to him. "Xavier, it is me. Baby, do you hear me." I told him softly. I couldn't imagine hurting him. But if I had to put him on his ass to get away, that was something that I was ready to do.

He pulled back and changed into the man. His eyes were still black and glaring at me. I didn't give a fuck about that. What I was seeing, was a naked Xavier with claws and bite marks all over his body. I was a healer, along with a lot of other shit. The shit that I was looking at on Xavier, looked fresh as shit.

I ignored his black eyes and heavy breathing. I went in on this fool. "Who the fuck did that to your body, nigga." I yelled. The blackness in his eyes dropped, and he was back to normal. But he was going to need whatever power he let go to get me to calm down. The house started shaking, lights were flicking, and the pipes were bursting. If I could lift this house up and sit that bitch on the moon, I would right now.

"Queen, it's not what you think." He tried to explain. Clearly, I wasn't trying to hear him or anything else that came out of his mouth. I steadied my breathing and thought of things that would fuck him up for a while. Could I make it hard for him to get it up, for the next check? Blue balls. Warts. Herpes. I knew that he wasn't going to suffer like the human men. I just wanted him to hurt like me. Fuck, something. He was still trying to reach me, but I was done.

I felt a breeze in my eyes. Not like the burning ones when I shift to my wolf. Xavier's mouth dropped open and everything went still. I tilted my head to the side and with one thought and no chants, every window, glass, TV screen, or anything else that was breakable, broke. Glass was flying everywhere. He didn't flinch or move. But, I believe whatever he saw freaked him out. I thought of the one place that Xavier didn't have access to and disappeared there. My room at my brother's was dark and cold. I pushed the images into my brother's head and they all responded with the same thing.

"We got you sis."

I got into my bed and cried. There was no thunder or lighting with it this time. Just a drizzle. It was enough to make me go to sleep and not think about the visions of the Guardian Facility.

TEN

Xavier

"Fuuck!" I yelled out. I knew I fucked up seriously. I had felt myself changing, and that was the reason why I had been staying away from Queen. Everything that she had been doing had been irritating the fuck outta me. I didn't know why at first, until I saw Chaos at night. I was becoming more in love with her, than my Queen. I didn't understand how this shit was possible, but it was happening.

I haven't touched Queen in a minute. I thought it was because I wanted her to heal so that she could get ready for me. That was bullshit. Just like Chaos was getting addicted to me, I was getting addicted to her. I wanted Queen to behave just like her and when she didn't, I became angry. But, what really fucked me up, was what Queen changed into. Her eyes turned white, and her hair was gold. She was fucking glowing, man. I was so stunned that I didn't realize she was gone until Nico walked in. He asked me where Queen was.

"She went to her brother's home. I'll put on some clothes and go check on her." I told him. Nico was looking around at the damages that my baby did. "I don't think that is a good idea. Maybe, you need to fall back. Let me go talk to her." Nico suggested.

I didn't need his help to fix shit. I knew he was going to side with her anyway. So, it really didn't make sense to tell him shit. And the way he was looking, I didn't think he wanted to hear it. "I don't." He said and walked out. I couldn't deal with his ass right now.

I went upstairs to put some clothes on. When I pulled my black joggers out, I saw that they were bleached. Matter fact, the whole room smelled like it. I walked into my closet and everything in that bitch was pink and purple.

"Aww, fuck no man. How the fuck did she do this?" I ran out the room and asked Xavion telepathically to have some clothes prepared for me.

I went back downstairs and out the back door. I shifted and ran to my brother's home. I couldn't believe I let things get this far. Chaos obeyed me and did everything I could have imagined doing. I wanted it to be with Queen, don't get me wrong. But, the way Chaos made me, and my wolf feel, had me craving for that dark pussy. I told her that she was only able to come out at night, or I was cutting her off. She complied and never made an appearance without me knowing.

I got to Xavion's house and he was sitting on the porch with clothes in his hands. "Do I even want to know why you need my clothes, when your closet is full like mine." He asked as I shifted back. I snatched the clothes from him and started putting them on.

Queen bleached my shit. Then she turned everything in my closet pink and fucking purple." I told him angrily. My sheriff uniform had bows and rainbows on them. I wasn't telling him that shit at all.

"She found scratches and bite marks on my body. Chaos gets real fierce during sex. Before I could tell her anything, Queen transformed into something different entirely. I thought that she was going to change into Chaos, but I was wrong." I sighed after putting on the shoes that Xavion gave me. "I don't know what to do."

"Maybe you should talk to her about it, Xavier." Xavion suggested.

"I am on my way to Dom's house now. Are you up for a fight right now?" I asked him. I was pretty sure that it was about to be one. She probably told them what she saw or gave them a visual. I knew Dom was going to give me hell, but not as much as Josh and Maxwell. They were going to fuck me up on sight.

"Yep. I didn't have anything else planned."

We jumped in his truck and headed to Nick's home. "What are you going to do when you get over there."

"I don't fucking know. I know that she is mad right now, but I gotta try something." I said.

"Well before you approach her, makes sure to tell her that those are my clothes, and my favorite shoes." Xavion told me.

"Shut the fuck up, bruh." I told him.

We pulled up to the house, and the brothers were sitting on the porch waiting for my arrival. It didn't surprise me to see that Nico was standing by the door blocking it. Xavion shook his head and jumped out the car with a smirk on his face. I got out and went straight to the Alpha of the pack. "Nick, it is not what you think."

"Please tell me that you have a good explanation for this shit. Because what I saw looked pretty fucked up." Nick said angrily.

"I tried to build a relationship with Chaos to get her to listen to me. We started fucking and things got wilder than what I'm used to." I told him, getting straight to the point.

They all looked up at each other and started laughing. I didn't find anything funny. I guess the shit was contagious, because Xavion started laughing too. "Why are you laughing? This shit was your idea." I told Xavion.

"Yeah but try to explain to Queen that you are cheating on her with her." He said laughing out loud again. The guys began to laugh as well. The shit did sound crazy. Nick recovered first and started talking.

"Do you control her." He asked.

"Somewhat. She hasn't been turning or flipping out on us, if you noticed." I told them, while having a seat next to him.

"That is true, but you see how that could fuck up things between you and my sister. She doesn't want Chaos to play a part in her life." Josh replied.

"I didn't know what to do, Josh. I mean she was blasting me through walls and shit." I told him.

"Yeah and now she is bleaching clothes and turning shit pink and purple." Xavion added.

"What the fuck are you talking about?" Maxwell asked. I didn't feel like explaining shit, so I showed them what I saw. Them fools started laughing some more.

"I gotta talk to her Nick." I ignored them.

"Come back tomorrow, Xavier. She is resting." Nico said.

"Yeah, come by tomorrow. She should be ok by then. In the meantime, let's go to the house and see these rainbow sheriff uniforms." Max said and continued laughing at the vision that I didn't want them to see.

ELEVEN

Patience

I was at my Nanny's house with my brother's wife and Jess. We were talking about the menu for the wedding and just some girl stuff. Nanny was baking some cookies, with some tea. I was a nervous wreck. I already talked to Jess about what happened, and she was going to talk to Xander about Xavier's behavior. We all sat around the table and Nanny started talking about me and Xavier's ceremony.

"It's not going to happen, Nanny. I think Xavier is cheating on me." I said to her. Everybody gasps in surprise.

"Patience, I don't think it is possible. It is physically impossible. If Xavier touches another woman, it would hurt him, physically." Nanny said.

"You're wrong, Nanny. Xavier is cheating on me. And we all know that he is more than just a wolf. His guardian side doesn't have to agree with his wolf side." I told them sadly. I wished that the shit was true. But, I know what I saw, and I wasn't going to let someone tell me I saw different.

"What did you see?" Treasure asked

"Bite marks and scratches, all over his body. His wolf also snapped at me when I tried to confront him about his fucked-up behavior. His eyes also turned black. I have never seen him like that." I told her. My Nanny was shaking her head in disbelief.

"What did he say when you confronted him about it?" Camryn asked.

"He told me that it's not what it seems." I whispered.

"I cannot believe my son would do some fuck boy shit like this. When I see his ass, I'm going to fuck his ass up myself." Nanny said pacing in her kitchen. We all stared at her and thought the same thing. She really needed to stop hanging out with my friends. Nanny was cursing and calling her son a whole fuck boy around here. She looked at us crazy. "Oh no, hunnie. Right is right and wrong is wrong over here. And when I see his ass, I'ma tell him about his self. Cuz, his father and I didn't raise him that way." Nanny continued with her rant. The girls were trying their hardest not to laugh at her.

"What are you going to do Patience? I mean, he already marked you." Treasure said. I looked over at Jess. She was the only one that knew what I did before coming over here. I pulled my shirt off my shoulder to show them.

"What the fuck?" Cam yelled out.

"Oh my god, Lil Bit. What have you done?" Nanny whispered with tears in her eyes. Treasure didn't say anything to me. The look of disappointment was written all over their face. I didn't care what no one thought. He wasn't about to claim me and fuck around with somebody else. So, I removed his mark. I am up for grabs, and many would know. His smell wasn't as strong as it was on me before. It was faint, and I couldn't wait for that bitch to go away.

"Patience, Xavier is going to fuck you up fa real." Cam told me.

"He can try, but I highly doubt it." I said, without a care in the world. I loved Xavier, but I loved me more.

Nanny was about to say something, but the front door opening interrupted her. We all knew who it was. My brothers told me that Xavier and I needed to talk. But, I didn't see it that way. So, I came to his mother's house where I knew he wouldn't start shit. At least I hoped.

The men walked into the kitchen, talking about some random shit. I picked up my empty glass and walked towards the sink. Even without his mark, I can feel him coming closer to me. I didn't want to be trapped between the sink and his body, so I turned and walked back to the kitchen island. When I passed Maxi, he took in my smell and frowned. "Why do you smell like fresh air?" He asked.

"What the fuck does fresh air smell like, Maxi?" I asked.

"It smells like you, shit. Don't be trying to play me. Cam and Treasure have all that air freshener shit in the house and that is what you smell like, our bathroom." He snapped.

"Maybe she smells like that because she stays there. It could have got on her clothes." Jess tried to cover for me.

"Yeah so does Cam and Treasure, but their mate's scent is still strong on them." Xavion said looking at me.

"Come here, Queen." Xavier said with anger boiling over each word.

I gave a sarcastic smirk and looked into his eyes. "I am not your Queen. Just like you are not my Alpha."

"Lil Bit..." Dom warned.

Xavier closed his eyes and sighed angrily. "They can't help you." He whispered out. "My mother or your brother's presences will not keep me calm, Queen. If you would have asked the right questions, you would have learned that magic cannot erase a mark of your mate. It's not there now, but it will reappear. You cannot escape this. We are forever." He told me and opened his eyes after. His breathing increased, and his wolf was itching to come out. His eyes were flashing from his wolf to that angry beast I encountered the other day.

"You see, Xavier, I have done my research and you are absolutely right. A Guardian's magic can't reverse a bite of a mate." I told him. He gave me that evil smirk, like he won. I shouldn't have continued, but the Alpha in me wouldn't let him win. "But...I am no ordinary Guardian." I told him with a smile of my own. "Checkmate."

His eyes went black completely and he rushed over to me. Dom, Maxi, and Josh jumped in front of me while Xander and Xavion held an out of control Xavier back. "You will always be mine! I don't give a fuck what you do! Any wolf, Guardian, or man that approach you, will die! I will kill them slowly in front of you! Fuck with it if you want!" He yelled out to me.

"Lil Bit go home." Dom told me. I knew he was disappointed in me as well. But I had to do what was right for me. I turned to leave the door, but it disappeared before my eyes. I turned around and was shocked to see Xavier in front of me.

"Holy shit! How did he get over there?" Xavion asked.

Dom tried to grab him, but Xavier disappeared again. When he reappeared this time, he was a wolf and came charging at me from another angle. Nico came out of nowhere in wolf form and charged at Xavier from the side. They went crashing out of the window. I made another door and walked out of it with the family behind me. Xavier and Nico were snapping and hitting each other with some heavy blows. Xavion, Xander, and Josh circled around them, while Dom and Maxi stayed with us.

"Take yo ass home right now." Dom said, looking directly at me. "Don't take no damn detours either."

I walked off the porch, leaving Nico and Xavier fighting, and walked into the woods. I was walking and thinking about what I wanted to do with my life. I was pretty sure that I was going to be leaving Louisiana for a while. It just wasn't the same anymore. The feeling I used to get when I came down here, was replaced with some fucked up memories. Aunt Lurita's death, my parent's death, and now a cheating ass mate. I was so done with this shit.

"Shit, I just want to get away for a while" I said to no one in particular.

"Tu peux aller où tu veux, Angel." (You can go wherever you want.) I heard a voice speak behind me. I turned around and saw a tall fit, cocoa complexion man. He looked older, but you know black folks age gracefully. He stood a few feet away from me and didn't make a move to come forward. He put me on pause calling me by the name that my mom and aunt used.

"Do I know you?" I asked. I felt my magic stirring inside of me and wanting to attack this man. I didn't want to attack him, and he was here to help. But, I haven't met a Guardian yet that wanted to help me. The only wolves I knew were in the pack of my brother's and Xavier's.

"Vous le faites, plus que vous ne le savez." (You do, more than you know.) He said, with his eyes changing all black. I didn't know why Xavier was the first person I thought of when I saw this. I didn't want his help for shit, so I called out for my brother. "Dom," I whispered. In less than a minute Xavier, Dom and Nico were there in front of me.

"What are you doing here?" Nico asked the stranger, that he apparently knew.

"I am getting so tired of people asking me that shit. What do you think I'm here for?" The man spoke in his James Earl Jones voice.

"You can't have her." Dom said shifting into his wolf. Xavier took my arm and placed me directly behind him. There was steam coming from Xavier's body.

"He won't have her." Xavier said in a voice that we all didn't recognize.

"None of you are in a position to tell me shit." The stranger said with eyes on me. "Tu me connais, Angel. Ouvre ton esprit et laisse ton grand-père entrer." (You know me, Angel. Open your mind and let your grandfather come in.)

"Don't do it Queen!" Nico yelled. The man chanted something, and Nico went flying. Dom stood still as our brothers attacked the man from behind. As soon as Maxi's wolf reached the man, he ran into an invisible force fill. Maxi bounced off it and flew back into a tree.

"Ne les laisse pas se blesser, Angel. Appelez vos chiens hors." Don't let them get hurt, Angel. Call your dogs off.) He spoke over the sounds my brothers were making trying to get through the force field.

I was still in shock about who he said he was. The last I heard was that he was dead, but he was trying to make peace before he disappeared to wherever he was at. I stared at him and saw my Aunt Lurita. She had his eyes and staring into them was fucking with me. But, this was the only person I had left from my mother's side. I really didn't want to miss this opportunity to get to know him and everything else about my mom and Aunt Lurita. He can teach me how to control my dark side.

"Angel," the man whispered.

Give him a chance Patience. "Grand-père".

He let down the force field, but I didn't let the guys know that I was ok with the man in front of me. Josh got through and his claws scratched my Grandpa's back. He turned around and hit Josh with a vicious blow. That shit set everybody in motion. Even Nico jumped in. Xavier stood next to me while our brothers attacked him. He sent them off one by one with lightening balls. He then approached me and Xavier. Xavier didn't let him say shit. He charged at my grandfather with his long claws. He tried to hit Xavier with the same lightening balls, but Xavier didn't fly back like the other guys. He absorbed it into his self. My Grandpa looked at Xavier and hit him with something that he couldn't absorb. The last thing I saw was Xavier flying backwards and spitting out blood.

TWELVE

Matteo

I have never seen anything more beautiful in my life. She was a mixture of her mother and father. But, that was my baby right there. She looked so much like Nesida when she was younger. The dark magic that was in her was running through her veins. She didn't have to learn it; it was a gift from me. And baby girl knew exactly how to use it.

She was surrounded by these wolves like they could protect her from me. Shit, I'm going to need them to protect me from her. I could have done a lot more damage to these frail ass dogs, but Angel loved them. I didn't come here to fight. We didn't have time for this shit. When I thought that I was getting somewhere, I let my guard down and one of the dog's claws got me in my back. I blasted them all a distance away from me. Nico and Angel's oldest brother attacked me and got in some good blows. I was surprised at them both. Her brothers had fight in them and that was good. I hit them with a blast and began to walk to Angel.

The one that was standing in front of her must have been her mate. He was growling and showing his teeth like I was some scared ass kid. He didn't give me a chance to say shit. He started swinging at me with his claws. I wasn't going to let him connect with any of those blows, so I hit him with the same electric ball as the others. But what fuck my head up was that this lil nigga took my shit in his soul. It was like he put that shit in his pocket for a rainy day. He started charging at me again, so I hit him with something stronger and that's when I felt the dark magic that woke me up at night.

I turned to face my Angel, who was now Chaos. Her black onyx hair and red eyes were looking straight through my soul. This is what I wanted for myself and Lurita. Now looking into the eyes of hell itself made me feel differently about wanting her with this power. My daughter created this child with love. There was no love in the eyes of this new being.

"Chaos, j'ai besoin de parler à ma petite-fille." (Chaos, I need to talk to my granddaughter.) I told her.

"Tu aurais dû y penser avant d'attaquer mon alpha." You should have thought about that before attacking my Alpha.) She spoke in a hollow voice.

"He attacked me." I told her getting angry. What was I supposed to do? Be her mate and brother's chew toy. Get the fuck out of here.

"That wasn't an attack. This. This is an attack, Papes." She told me. I kept my eyes on her lips to read out her chants, but her lips didn't move. She raised her hand up and vines came up from the ground and wrapped around my body.

"Angel, I am here to help you. Stop this now." I demanded.

She smiled at me and shook her head no. Nico came back in view with the others. I heard him tell her mate and brothers that they should listen to what I had to say. One of the poodles suggested I become plant food for the *Little Shoppe of Horror* plant that she created. I heard someone smack the back of his head, while the vines started to swallow me in. I didn't want to attack her, because it was only going to antagonize her more. "He wasn't trying to attack y'all. The only reason why Josh got him was because Lil Bit called him Grandpa." The oldest brother said. They all looked over at me.

"You can come and help me any fucking day now." I told them.

Her mate walked over to her and began caressing her face. "Tha hell," I said. She was letting him pet her like she was the dog. I got loose from the vines and focused on calling all my dark magic back. Chaos looked up to me and saw what I was doing. It was too late for her to try anything, because Angel was standing in her place.

She looked confused at first. But when she saw that her mate was holding her, she pushed him out of his arms. "Stay the fuck away from me, Xavier." She told him and walked towards me slowly. I waited for her to come and ask all of the questions that were building up in her head.

Angel was standing in front of me now, staring. "Salut," she said softly. I chuckled at her greeting. I gave in and grabbed her into a hug. She didn't respond to the hug at first, until she felt the sadness and joy that I was feeling.

"Bonjour mon doux petit ange." (Hello, my sweet little angel.) I pulled back to get a better look at her. "Je suis fière de toi. Vous avez tenu et a été assez fort pour survivre à la fois sombre et la lumière. Savez-vous que vous avez accompli quelque chose que les gens ont essayé de comprendre depuis des années?" (I'm so proud of you. You are and was strong enough to survive both dark and light. DO you know that you have accomplished something that people have been trying to understand for years.) I told her in awe.

"No Grandpa, I don't know. Maybe you can teach me and tell me some other things that I don't know about our family." She asked.

"N'importe quoi pour toi, Angel." (Anything for you, Angel.) I pulled her in for another hug and kissed her on the top of her head the same way I used to do to my babies. "Rien." (Anything.)

~

We got to her family's house, where introductions were made. They were still skeptical about me, but I didn't care. I wasn't here to get their approval. Better yet, her mate better hope that I give my ok with this mating shit.

"So, you can control her dark magic." Her mate's youngest brother asked.

"Yes, for now. It took a lot of energy to do that. She is much stronger than I am. If she is distracted, then I can push it back into her temporarily." I directed my attention to Angel.

"What type of nightmares have you been having?" I asked her. I didn't want to come out and tell her what I already know and trigger some shit in her head. I had to find out what she knew, so that we can go forward with a plan.

"I don't want to talk about that right now." She said getting up. Xavier jumped up in front her and stopped her in her tracks.

"Why didn't you tell me about your nightmares, Queen?" He said with concern. I knew it wasn't my place to jump into their conversation. But, like I said I didn't give a fuck about nobody's feeling but my little Angel.

"How you not know about your mate's nightmare? Don't you spend the night with each other and shit? The nightmares that she had would have brought her out of her sleep into tears. Where the fuck was you?" I asked. I haven't had the opportunity to boss up on my girl's first date or boyfriends. Angel was my baby now and I was going to give this nigga hell.

"Probably out fucking some stupid bitch, while I was sleep-walking into shit." She said and pushed off of him again. If she was anything like her mother and grandmother, nature wouldn't let anything happen to her if she was sleepwalking into the woods. That was how she was able to get from the house that she shared with her Aunt Lurita. Someone tried to kidnap her on the way to her favorite tree. My Angel took the muthafucker's head off with a left hook. She was making me proud all around.

He looked at me and didn't say nothing. Something wasn't right with this situation. He did absorb my dark magic during our little fight. I looked around at everyone else and for some reason they all were ignoring the elephant in the room. I thought about it some more and came up with my own solution. I was going to let this go for now. We had more important shit to go over.

"Angel, we need to know. These are not nightmares, and you know that. They are memories of Chaos. In so many ways, she is trying to tell you what happened."

She sighs and sits next to her brother Maxi. "I don't want to see what she did." She told me. She looked… scared. Xavier walked over and kneeled in front of her. He tried to grab her hand, but she yanked it from him.

"Whatever it is, you don't have to fear shit, Queen. I wouldn't let anything happen to you." He told her. He was trying his best to get back on good terms with her. But the stubbornness in her wasn't going to let whatever go at that moment.

"Yeah, Xavier. You wouldn't let anything happen to me. Riiight, because you're doing everything. Get the fuck out of my face before I kick you in the throat." She told him and rolled her eyes at him.

"Do what you gotta do, Queen." He replied. We were interrupted by the phone. Dominick's mate went to answer it.

"Angel, we need to know about the memories. Chaos got a lot of information from the Supreme that was at that facility." I told her.

"I don't see much, Papi. Everything goes blurry after I took out the guards at the facility." She told me.

"Hey, sorry to interrupt, but they need y'all at the facility." Dominick's mate said.

"Did they say why?" Dominick asked.

"No, they just need y'all at the station." She told them.

"We are going to check this out right quick. We'll be back to discuss this." Xavier told Patience. She ignored his ass like he wasn't there. He leaned in to kiss her and she pulled back in disgust. He turned towards Nico and told him not to let her out of his sight. He then turned towards me. I knew what he was about to ask me, so I beat him to it.

"Let's go."

I got up and went to stand in the middle of the room. I looked over at my Angel, who looked confused. "I'll be right back, Angel." They all placed a hand on me and we all were teleported to the front of the sheriff's station. We walked in and there were men standing at the front desk. They looked like a bunch of raggedy muthafuckers. A man walked ahead of the group and directed his attention to Xavier.

"I, Kevin Sporiles, challenge you for your position and to mate with the daughter of the Nesida." He told him. I looked around, like I was in the twilight zone. Is this shit really happening?

"Hold the fuck up." I interrupted. "Your people called us to the station for this bullshit." I asked in disbelief.

"Yeah. X and Lil Bit are not properly mated yet. Until then, he will be challenged." Xavier's brother explained to me. This was one of the main reasons why I didn't respect wolves and their pack laws. If this was some shit that my family worked hard for, how is it that a bum ass nigga gon' try to challenge me for some shit that ain't theirs?

"I have a question." I raised my hand like I was in school. "How is it that you claimed my granddaughter to be your Queen, but you are about to fight this water head ass white boy for her."

"Until we are properly mated, I will be challenged for my land and her hand." He spat that same shit as his brother. The shit still had me confused. They started walking outside and I stopped them again.

"So, you and my granddaughter are not destined to be together." I asked.

He turned around with a scowl on his face. "She is mine." He growled out with black eyes. Aww, nah, I get it. This stupid ass boy been taking energy from Chaos. This shit was getting crazier by the minute.

"If she is yours, dismiss this shit. We got better things to do with our time. We have to prepare for a war. If you need a sparring partner, I will gladly create one for you." I said looking over at his opponent. "Cuz I don't see him lasting long."

"We abide by pack laws around here. I am the Alpha of my pack. What would it look like if I go against everything that was taught to me? Huh? I would look like a fucking hypocrite." He said.

"You're wrong, Xavier." I told him. I can't believe this weak ass lil nigga wanted to be with my baby. He was going to have to show me different. "You need to man up and object to this shit or something."

"How you figure? He can't just not accept the challenge." His other brother asked.

82

"Xavier is not just wolf. He is of another breed. Just like my granddaughter. You don't have rules made for you. You make your own." I told him. He stood stunned on his feet. I knew he had been living as a wolf his whole life. But he was part Guardian, too. Angel was rejecting Chaos, and Xavier was rejecting his Guardian side. They were the perfect confused couple. I walked over to his opponent and his stupid ass tried to stand taller than what he was. "You want to fight." I asked him.

"Yes, I came here to challenge him." He said out loud.

"Good," I told him. I touched the two guys that were standing next to him and chanted. The two guys turned towards their leader with black eyes. "Here you go." I said and turned back around. They jumped on him and started whipping his ass. Everybody was looking at me crazy. "Like I told y'all young asses, we got shit to do."

THIRTEEN

Xavier

*J*was sitting here listening to Queen's grandfather. He told us what he stumbled on in Tennessee at the Southern Guardian facility. I can't believe that she could do something like that. We were trying to come up with strategies that will keep her safe. But there was nothing that we could prepare ourselves for. We may have the strength to deal with a Guardian in hand to hand combat and survive, but if they used magic against us, we will lose.

I went to Dom's house and slept in one of the rooms that he had downstairs. I wanted to go to my Queen so bad. Her stupid ass grandfather put a spell on her door. When I touched it, it shocked the fuck out of me. You could hear him laughing outside, along with Nico.

We were now sitting at my mother's home for a rehearsal dinner. Xander and Jess' mating ceremony was on tomorrow. We had guests coming from different packs later to celebrate with us. The women had a nice spread laying in front us. The girls were going to New Orleans and the guys were going to play some poker and some other shit.

"Ms. Noelle, this gumbo is so good." Loreen told her.

"Oh, thank you, baby. I'll put some up for you to take home." My mother told her. She was always making to-go plates for somebody.

I was sitting across from Queen. She hasn't looked or talked to me all day. I was getting annoyed with this whole cheating shit. Then she got real bold and erased my mark. She just didn't know, I was going to be marking her ass every night if she kept playing with me.

"Y'all, I am so ready to get this party on the road." Tori said and looked at my mom. "Ms. Noelle, you should come with us. You not doing nothing after this anyways."

"Child please, I have so much shit to do. I gotta make sure the food and the menu are on point. We have guests coming in from the north and from out west." She told her while standing up with her plate. "Besides, y'all don't want me out there showing y'all lil girls out." She laughed.

"Oh, I know you lying." Jess said. She looked over at Queen and peeped out her mood. "What's wrong P?" She asked the question that I been waiting to ask for a minute now. I knew that she was either going to curse me out or just ignore me.

"I don't think that it would be good if I go out tonight. You know, with everything that has been happening." She said in a whisper.

"You have been good, though. She hasn't popped up in a minute. For once, let's just have fun and not worry about nothing. You deserve some fun time, P." Jess told her. Everyone nodded their heads in agreement, but she was still doubtful.

"Angel, if you are having so many problems control her, ask Xavier. It seems that he has a close relationship with her." Queen's grandfather said.

And dropped mic.

It seemed like everybody's spoon stopped midair after that comment. I didn't know what kind of game her grandfather was playing, but this was fucked up on so many levels. I felt Queen's eyes on me.

"Aww shit," Maxi mumbled and stood. "Well, dinner was good. See y'all at the spot." He said walking towards the door.

"Sit the fuck down, Maxi." Queen said with her eyes burning in my own. Maxi sat quickly but pulled his seat from the table. She was shaking her head, trying to calm herself down. "So, that's why your wolf was snapping at me, cuz I wasn't that bitch!" She yelled. I tried to talk but she shut that shit down by holding up her hand. "You been fucking her this whole time. Wow! You are seriously fucked up for that, fa real!"

"Oh, hell naw! What's the bitch name?" Her friends jumped up and asked. Maxi's stupid ass, knowing that Chaos and Queen was the same person, still encouraged their ratchet ass behavior.

"That bitch name is Chaos." Maxi said.

"Chaos. So, you want a troublesome bitch. Ok. Well tell that hoe Chaos that we about to bring that mayhem to her ass. Nah, fuck that shit, Xavion. Don't be trying to calm nothing down over here. You and yo pussy ass brother probably knew that he was fucking around on my girl." Loreen said.

The guilty look on his face, along with the others proved her point. Jess yanked back from Xander and went to stand by a pissed off Queen. "I can't believe you would do this to me." Queen whispered. I heard the hurt and the disappointment in her voice.

"What did I do Queen? I built a relationship with your other half. With you! You make it seem like I am out here fucking some random chick." I told her.

"She is not me, so that makes her random! I am not like that. I don't do the shit she has done, and for you to say that, goes to show how much you know me." She said and stood up.

"The fuck is you talking about? She is you. How the fuck I cheat on you, with you? Like I said, I built a relationship with her and she listens to me. She didn't come out the other day when you were talking about your Aunt Lurita to Jess. She didn't come out when you were talking to my mom about your parents in the kitchen. We have an understanding. You would too, if you would stop trying to find a way to get rid of her and listen." I yelled.

"You have an understanding." She says mockingly. "What is our understanding, Xavier? Keep secrets. Plan shit about me, and not tell me. I have been growing weaker and weaker, and I didn't know why." She laughed while wiping the tears from her eyes. "You are giving her another reason to take over me. I woke up every morning with new bruises and wounds. You had me thinking that I was sleep-walking! Oh My God! You could have told me that the both of you was fucking at night. What makes the shit even worse, you think that you have control over her, but you don't. She has been feeding you her energy, dumb ass. That was why your eyes went black. She has bonded with your wolf." She said and shook her head. Queen looked over at her brothers. "You guys was supposed to have my back. Why?" She said with more tears running down her face. She looked at Maxi and he put his head down in shame. "Not you. Please tell me, that you didn't know nothing about this?" She whispered. Maxi couldn't pick his head up and lie to her face.

Tori and Loreen looked around for someone to explain what was going on. Jess put her hands on her shoulder to try and calm her down. The women were looking at me in disgust. My own mom was ready to swing on me. Tori and Loreen walked over to Queen. "Don't worry about that shit. Let's just hocus pocus his ass and get the fuck out of here." Tori said while staring at me with her stank face. Queen started walking off with them, and I wasn't having it. I caught her at the end of the table and blocked them from leaving.

"Let me talk to you for a minute." I told her.

"You had many minutes to tell me about this shit, Xavier." She said and tried to walk around me. I grabbed her arm and pulled her back to me. She stared up at me, and what I saw was amazing. Her eyes were white, and her body was glowing. "It would be in your best interest, if you let me go." She told me in an angelic voice. Totally opposite from what I thought I would hear. My mom came behind me and pulled me back.

"Thank you, Nanny." She said and walked out the door with the girls. Nico and her grandfather walked out behind them shaking their heads. Camryn turned towards Josh. "Did you know?" She asked him. Josh let out a deep breath and answered with a head nod. Camryn was six months pregnant right now. But, the way she jumped out that chair and snapped at him, had us all taking a step back.

"Baby, look, I'm sorry I didn't tell you." He told her.

"What fucking ever, Josh." She said while waiting at the end of the table.

Treasure shook her head and began to get up as well. "I'm not even going to ask you that question." She told Nick. Nick grabbed her hand to pull her back down into her seat.

"Naw, fuck that Treasure. That shit doesn't have anything to do with us." He told her.

Treasure pulled her hand out of Nick's and stared him in the eyes. "When my sister is hurting, then I'm hurting. When I'm hurting," she paused and placed her hand on his dick and continued. "You're hurting. Fix it." She said and walked to the end of the table to Camryn. They both walked outside with the other girls.

"Fuck that, X. Go out there and fix this shit. I ain't going without my mate because yo simple ass fucked up." Nick exploded.

"Fa real, X. Fix that shit." Josh said equally angry.

I turned to face my mom. "Why did you pull me back? Is there somebody else inside of her that I need to know about?" I asked curiously.

"Why you want to know? So, you can fuck her into submission too. I ain't telling you shit." My mom told me and walked off.

Nick, Josh, and Xander walked up to me and stared. "What," I asked.

"What the fuck do you mean what? My mating ceremony is tomorrow. I don't want Jess to think that I had anything to do with this, man. We are going to New Orleans and yo ass is going to tell her that I had nothing to do with this." He told me.

"Fa real. Jess got a pastor coming out here and everything. When he asks does anyone object to this marriage, she might raise her own got damn hand." Xavion added.

"Aww fuck, man. Come on, Xavier. You got to make this shit right. I told you not to do this shit. Fuck!" Xander yelled over and over. I knew that he was nervous about the mating ceremony. But, he knew damn well that Jess was going to marry his stupid ass.

88

"Calm down. You know that you and Jess are meant to be, man." I told him.

"That is not the fucking point, X. We are not mated like Josh and Dominick. Our women are mad without mating marks." He said. That shit had me jumping in the SUV with the guys. I wish she fucking would.

FOURTEEN

Patience

*M*uthafucker. I was extremely pissed. I couldn't believe that this nigga was fucking her crazy ass. I told him how weak I was getting, and his ass didn't say shit. She was trying to get out to be with Xavier. Shit started making sense. He basically came home when it was time to go to bed. I was more pissed off with him not talking to me about his plan. We could have come up with something together. But he went to my brothers or his brothers and got advice. Stupid ass advice.

We were now on Bourbon Street, getting fucked up. Camryn and Treasure were standing around the circle that was created around us. We were dancing to that Anita Baker, *No One in the World*, with that DJ Act Right beat. We were singing, and the girls were getting lit. I was never able to let go and have fun like that. I was the one that was always on guard and ready to protect my girls if need be. Not now. I was tooting and backing it up. I didn't fucking care. My Papi and my Godfather were here to protect us. It was my time to have fun.

Lurita came and grabbed my hand. She held it up and showed me off. The guys were trying to get my attention, but I didn't want to be bothered. Anita Baker went off and Betty Wright, *After the*

Pain, with that beat was next. I was singing that shit and doing that New Orleans step. The one where you got your Daiquiri in one hand, in the air and your other hand empty, so you can snap to that beat. Yeah y'all. I was feeling this shit.

Some random ass dude came behind me and started dancing on me. Loreen nodded her head to let me know that he was ok looking. I just kept my back turned. I didn't know how close the bitch was to Xavier, but she was going to sit her ass down somewhere. No dick for you bitch. I wasn't fucking with her tonight. Shit, she was going to let me do me.

I picked my head up and saw that Dom and Josh were with Cam and Treasure. I looked to my left and Maxi was grinding on some chick. Xander was in the corner trying to explain the situation to Jess. I already knew that Tori was at the bar getting more shots. I looked back at Loreen and Xavion was behind the dude that was dancing on her. I heard Xavier growl loudly behind me.

I didn't let that stop me from dancing, but the dude behind me was more than finished. "My bad dawg, I didn't know that she was here with somebody." He told Xavier. The man walked over to where his friend was and grabbed him from behind Loreen. "Nigga, what you doing? Go back over there and dance with that beauty." He told his friend.

My old dance partner looked back at me and shook his head. "Nah bruh, the dude behind me growled bruh. He didn't speak, he growled. That shit came from within. Fuck that. They got a lot of women in this bitch." He told him. The dude wasn't letting up though. He looked at Xavion and his stupid ass flashed his wolf eyes at him. The dude stepped back in shock. He tapped his friend shoulder again. "Bitch let's go. I don't know if he's Vampire on Bourbon or what. But I am not about to be on the First 48." He walked off with his boy trailing right behind him after Xavion let out a growl of his own. "Did he just call me a vampire?" Xavion asked.

"Me and you not even like that. What the fuck?" Loreen asked him.

"We can be." He told her and licked his lips.

Loreen looked back at me. If I told her that I was still mad at Xavier, she would have dismissed Xavion. But I knew my girl wanted him and I wasn't going to block that. She been holding out on Xavion. She didn't want to be his mate or anything. She was looking for a bedmate. I nodded my head to give her the okay and the smile on the hoe face could have been placed on the Colgate commercial. There was no need for everybody to be upset.

I was about to go and tell Jess to stop acting bad with Xander, when Xavier grabbed my waist and pulled me into his body. I knew that I was mad and all, but fuck. For some reason, my body was craving him even more. His smell. His touch. His voice. I was about to lose my fuckin mind on the dance floor. He brought his lips closer to my ear and whispered into it. "So, that's the type of shit you do. You get mad and let these men touch and watch what's mine."

The roughness in his voice had me looking for the nearest exit. How can I be like fuck Xavier in one minute, then fuck me Xavier in the next? I tried to take a step forward, but his grip got tighter. "Queen, don't get fucked up in here. I told you before that you are mine. I love every fucking part of you. I accepted every part of you." He said, then turned me around to face him. "You mad, be mad. But if you ever say that I am not your Alpha again," he paused, and his eyes flashed white.

I began to gain control over my body and express to him how I felt. He had to know that what I was feeling, was because of his stupid ass plan. "If you are my Alpha, why make the decision you made about me, without me? You told me that I can talk to you about anything. Did you tell me that, so that you can get closer to her? Because at this point, Xavier, I don't trust you." I told him.

He shook his head and grabbed me by my throat. "I'm sorry that I didn't tell you about the plan, alright. If I can do the shit over, I would. All this shit is new to the both of us. I was desperate to do whatever it took to keep her from popping up the way she was doing. Queen," he leaned his forehead on mine and whispered my name. "Forgive me, baby."

Oh, my damn. I felt the juices leaking through my thong. Everything in me wanted to forgive him, but I couldn't. I pulled back and looked up at him. "I gotta go," I responded. He snatched my hand and brought me back to his body.

"You ready to go, that's fine, but we are leaving together." He told me and led me out the door. Everyone followed behind us. We went to a bigger house on St. Charles in New Orleans. Xavier was trying to lead me into one of the bedrooms on the third floor, but I declined.

"Xavier, I need time. You betrayed me, whether you want to believe it or not. Respect my wishes and leave me alone."

He took a deep breath and sighed. "I am not letting you go, Queen." He told me straight up. "But if you need time to figure out shit, you got that. I'll wait. I'll wait forever for you, Queen." He leaned forward and placed a kiss on my lips. He walked off leaving me to my thoughts. I went into the room and tried to figure out my next move. Clearly, Chaos felt that her connection with Xavier was stronger than mine. I had to set this hoe straight real quick.

∿

We all woke up the next morning with a lot of shit to do. I had to pick up Jess's mother and brother from the airport. On the ride to the house, we discussed a lot of her concerns. She didn't want to talk about them with Jess. She heard how happy her daughter was and didn't want to fuck that up. She asked if Jess's little brother, Jeff should be there. I told her that it would be wise if he left after the ceremony was over. Jess told her mom, but they both decided to tell Jeff when he get older. That was why Jess had the minister there. She wanted to make it look like a normal wedding.

We got to my brother's house thirty minutes after I picked them up from the airport. Xander and the rest of the men were at his mom's house getting ready. When we walked in, all the women were sitting in the family room talking about what will happen at the ceremony.

"Mommy!" Jess yelled and ran over to her mom.

"Hey, Ms. Rye, you are looking good." Tori said while walking towards her.

"Girl, she dressed up like she about to get married." Loreen joked, after hugging her.

"Well y'all know I gotta look good too." She replied. I introduced her to Treasure and Camryn. My grandfather walked in with Nico, from the kitchen.

"Ms. Robin, this is my Grandfather Matteo." He reached out and gave her a hug. We were all surprised by his actions. He pulled back and smiled. "You took care of my baby with my daughter. You accepted her into your family and treated her like your own. I, thank you, Robin Rye." He told her and patted me on top of my head as he passed by. I was about to introduce Nico to Ms. Robin. Nico's eyes were glowing.

"Holy shit!"

FIFTEEN

Xavier

I can't believe that bullshit Queen's grandfather tried to pull at the dinner. He knew that she didn't know what was going on with me and Chaos. He was a bitch fa that. I wanted to tell him about that shit, but I was going to wait until after the ceremony was over. I didn't want to fuck up my brother's day.

When I saw Queen dancing in the club with some random ass dude, I had to hold back all the rage that was threatening to come through. She was really testing my Alpha. I was going to give her the time she needed to think about whatever. But, what she didn't know, was that she was going to be doing all her thinking under the roof of our home. Fuck all that bullshit.

My mom got our attention when she walked in with her gown on. My mother was a beautiful woman. She was shorter than us, of course. But the fire in her eyes, made you feel small as shit. She had tears in her eyes looking at the men she raised. We were all dressed in a beige custom-made linen suit. Hand stitched shirts, with some Brooks Brothers hazelnut loafers. The shit fitted nicely on us. We usually had to get all our clothes custom made due to our sizes.

"My babies are now men. I am so proud of you all." She turned and faced Xander. Tears of happiness were rolling down her face. "Your father would have been so proud of you, Andy." She said and pulled him into a hug. Xavion walked over to join them in their embrace. I stood back and watched my family. My mother looked up at me. "I know that you don't think that you are too old to join us." Mom said. I walked over and hugged them all.

My mother walked out to give us time to ourselves. There was no kind of advice that I could give to Xander about relationships. He was doing better than me in that department right now. Xander was pacing a little bit. He looked worried. I looked over at Xavion and his ass was laughing on the slick. I knew he wasn't worried about Jess responding negatively to mating words. Queen already let the girls know that all the men were forgiven, but me.

"What's wrong, Andy?" I asked him while stepping in front of his walking path.

"Nothing, bruh. I am ready to make Jess mine. We gotta go through all this shit before we go into the woods. Then, I know for a fact that my baby is going to look good. These thin ass pants ain't holding my shit down. Man, Mom is going to be out there, along with my mother-in-law, seeing my dick all hard and shit. Man, it's embarrassing." He told us.

Xavion busted out laughing. I didn't know what to say. I didn't think of that at all. I knew that I was going to be hard as fuck, waiting to mate with Queen. Mom was going to have to turn her head. I didn't think that I will make it all the way through the ceremony myself.

"Hey, just give us a sign or something, when you feel like you can't hold on anymore. We will step in and take care of things." I told him.

"What the fuck are we supposed to do? Tell everybody to close their eyes until Lil Andy get his pecker under control." Xavion said, still laughing at Xander. We all started laughing. Dom and the rest of the brothers walked in and congratulated Xander. It was rare that we find a mate in a human. Some of the members in our packs had mated with other wolves that weren't their mate, because they didn't have the luck that we had.

Someone knocked on the door, and Josh went to open it. It was a woman and a teenaged boy standing in the doorway. Xander walked forward and kissed her on the cheek. "Hi Ms. Robin, how was your trip?" Xander asked her.

"It was good, Xander. I wanted to come and see you first, before you become my son-in-law." She pulled back and smiled. But, then her smile dropped, and she started mugging Xander. Xander stood his ground and looked her in the eyes. "If you fuck over my daughter, Xander King. I will skin you and use you for a rug." She said, menacingly.

"Fair enough, Ms. Robin, but there is no need for the threat. Jessica will always come first in my life. I would die before I hurt her and kill anyone who tries." He told her with his wolf eyes showing.

"Good," she told him not backing down.

Xander stepped up to the boy and shook his hand. "Hey Jeff, what's good with you, bruh."

"Nothing. Please take care of my sister for me." He told him.

"You got that, lil man." Xander replied. They walked out and Xander turned towards us. "Yo, you think Jess mom used to be something else in her past life." He asked us.

We all started laughing at his dumb ass. There was another knock on the door, letting us know that the ceremony was about to start. Nick, Josh, and Maxi left me and Xavion alone with Xander.

"I'm proud of you man." I told him.

I gave him another hug. Xavion did the same and walked out the door. The mating ceremony was always supposed to be held at night, underneath the moon and the stars. There were chairs lined up on the left and right. The chairs were white with gold sashes hanging from them. They also had a gold runner in the middle of the aisle. Mom made us grab the old arc out back. It was made from vines and beautiful white and gold lilies.

We walked up the aisle one by one, with Xander being the last one. We stood next to a pastor and Elder Locklear. Jess' family were there on the left and our pack members, along with some of Dom's pack were sitting on the right. You could hear the women in Jess' family complementing our looks and attire. I swear I heard one of them say that we couldn't hide that print fa shit. Xavion's stupid ass ate that shit up. I just hoped that they kept that shit to themselves when my Queen walked out here. I knew she was still mad, but she wouldn't let no one say some shit like that about me.

Soft music began to play. That was the signal for the girls to walk out. Xander didn't want to walk to any music. He said that was the women shit. Tori and Loreen walked out, beige dresses with no straps, short in the front and long in the back. Xavion was drooling staring at Loreen. She flirted back with him by licking her lips. That fool had to turn his back on the crowd to hide his shit. Xander smiled at his action. "You are an ass for that. How you gon' brick up like that at my ceremony, bruh? Get yo shit together." He teased him.

I started laughing with him until I saw my Queen coming down the aisle. She had on the same dress, but she was fitting her shit. Queen was glowing in the moonlight. Her skin looked smooth and soft. Her breasts were sitting up nice and plump. She had her hair swooped to the side which left the shoulder that was marked, visible. Everyone saw that she was now available. Since everyone was family, I didn't have anything to worry about. She looked up at me and I could have sworn that her eyes were glowing. I took a step forward, but Xavion pulled me back.

"Bruh, calm yo shit. You over here growling and shifting." He told me. I couldn't take my eyes off of her. It was like her body was calling out for me.

She must have felt the pull as well, because she started walking towards me, biting on her bottom lip. I yanked my arm away from Xavion and was meeting her halfway. My mother and Queen's grandfather jumped in the middle of us.

"You two wait 'til it's your turn. Right now, this time belongs to Xander and Jessica." She told both of us. Queen's grandfather gave her a slight shove, while Mom pushed me back into my spot.

"I'm sorry Xander. I didn't mean to lose control like that on your day." I told him, when I got back into my spot.

"Don't worry about it, X. I know the pull of the moon isn't making it better for the both of you." He replied with understanding. He wasn't lying. The moon was calling out for me to take Queen into the woods and mate her. I took in a deep breath and concentrated on being here for my brother. A different song came on and Jess began to walk down the aisle with her little brother Jeff. She was wearing a cream off the shoulder linen dress. It had a long split in the middle of it. When she walked, her leg slipped out, and that had Xander growling. The pastor looked over to us, in fear.

"We hungry over here, Pastor. Let's get this over with so that we can grub it up." Xavion stepped forward and told him. I didn't trust myself to say shit. I was still calming down from Queen's scent.

The pastor began to go through the original ceremony. "Who giveth this woman to be married to this man?" He asked out loud.

"I do," her brother said. He gave her a kiss and placed her hand into Xavier's. When their hands touched, Xander's breathing became heavy. I spoke up this time, because clearly Xander wasn't going to make it to the end.

"Hey pastor, we gotta skip to the part where they speak their own vows." I told him in a rush. He just nodded his head and stepped back to let Elder Locklear continue.

"Ok, Xander and Jess, speak your truths." Elder Locklear told them.

Jess looked into my brother's eyes and spoke her truth. "I, Jessica Rye, will give all that I am to Xander King. I will be your moon during the day and your stars to guide you home. I will follow your lead and trust your word. I will keep my womb filled with your sons and daughters, to carry on your legacy. I am yours Xander King."

Xander began to speak right after the last word came out of Jessica's mouth. "I, Xander King, will give all that I am to Jessica Rye. I will be your moon during the day and your stars to guide you home. I will lead by example and show you that I can be trusted. I will keep your womb filled with sons and daughters, to carry on the King legacy. I am yours Jessica Rye."

"With the blessing from the family and the bright moon above. You are now mated. Congratulations, Xander and Jessica King." Elder Locklear told them. Xander wasted no time. He picked Jessica up and ran into the woods with her. Jess' family was surprised that

Xander didn't kiss Jessica after they spoke their truths. If he did, they would have gotten a very inappropriate show. The pastor was looking stunned by Elder Locklear's words.

"Mated," he whispered. Xavion and I walked off from that. We didn't want to have to explain shit to the pastor.

Everyone got up and started walking to the food. I stood back and waited for them to leave to get Queen's attention. She tried to ignore me but that pull that I was feeling, wasn't coming from the moon. I grabbed her arm when she tried to walk past me.

"Queen, can we go somewhere and talk." I asked her.

"Not now, Xavier. Let's celebrate with the family. And you promised me, that you were going to give me some time. It hasn't been a full twenty-four hours yet." She replied, while her head was down. She was trying to distance herself from me. I pulled her to me and grabbed her hair. I pulled it back, so that she could see how serious I was.

"I love you, Queen." I told her right before I pressed my lips to hers softly. I pulled back and her eyes were still closed from the kiss. "Save me a dance, please." I whispered.

She smiled up at me and opened her hazel eyes. "I can do that." She told me. She walked off, with me watching. Fuck! My Queen was the most beautiful thing that was created. I walked towards the food and the guests. Tori and Loreen thought that it would have been a good idea to have a DJ. Xander told them that it was fine, but he didn't want none of that bounce music at their ceremony. Loreen and Tori rolled their eyes and called us bougie. "What the fuck do you want us to play Xander? Who let the dogs out?" She asked. We all started laughing.

Two hours later, and the DJ was playing RnB and some appropriate rap songs. Jessica's mom didn't like all that shit either. Speaking of Ms. Robin, Nico been on her back since she got here. I was about to ask Dom about that when Queen's grandfather walked up to me.

"This was a great ceremony." He told me. I didn't know where he was going with this. "Yeah, it was. I can't wait for me and Queen to have our ceremony. Will you be giving her away?"

"Not to you." He told me in a calm voice. "You see Xavier, my little Angel needs someone that can trust her. Apparently, you didn't after holding in a secret like that." He said to me. I knew this muthafucker didn't come over here for small talk.

"So, that's why you brought that shit up at my mother's dinner table. You think that your Angel won't forgive me and move on to some Harry Potter muthafucker." I told him. "He wouldn't last a day with my Queen. No one will. She was made for me and I was made for her. She's not going nowhere, Grandpa."

"Please lil nigga. You don't intimidate me by flashing your white eyes and pointy teeth, boy. I am what you should fear. Believe dat." He said while standing a foot from me. I shook my head after seeing what I knew from the jump.

"I don't fear no man."

"I am not just a man, boy." He said, taking that last step forward. We were standing toe to toe. I was four inches taller than him, but grandpa didn't let that scare him.

"You are right. You are more than a man, Lord of the Darkness. But your darkness, don't have shit on my Queens. I felt and tasted the darkness in my Queen. You ain't shit compared to her." I told him. You can see that he looked ok with Queen being stronger than him. He just didn't like the way I put it out for him. His eyes started to change, and he was getting ready to attack.

"Papi, not here, not now. Go take a walk and cool down." Queen told him. He looked towards her and nodded his head.

"Ok, Angel," he replied and walked off, without a backwards glance.

I looked over to Queen and she continued talking to some of Jessica's cousins. Nick and the rest of the men came over to talk to me. "You keep fucking with Grandpa, and he gon' fuck you up." Nick said.

"Fuck him. He started that shit at the table. I didn't want to bring that up today, but his punk ass walked over here talking shit. He said that our mating ceremony wasn't going to happen." I growled. I felt myself getting angry. I was ready to shift and hunt his ass down.

Josh was about to speak but the howl of a wolf interrupted him. We all howled back to congratulate my brother. The guests were looking at us crazy, like we lost our fucking mind. We didn't pay them no mind. My brother was a mated man. This was something to howl about.

SIXTEEN

Patience

$\mathcal{I}$ watched everyone have a great time at my best friend's mating ceremony. Papi and Xavier have been mugging each other ever since the secrets were brought out at the dinner. I was over it. I knew that I wasn't going anywhere. If so, Xavier would have dragged me back home and punished me well. Thinking about those punishments had me ready to climb his big ass.

I didn't know what the hell happened when I walked down the aisle. Something was stirring inside of me and pushing me to go to Xavier. When Papi jumped in front of me, and told me to calm down, I tried to pull my magic in. Chaos was reaching out to Xavier. I felt her slipping through. I called out to my wolf and she shut that shit down. She wanted Xavier too, but she was uncomfortable with Chaos or any other magic running the show.

"Hey P, you want to dance." Jess' cousin Maurice asked, bringing me out of my thoughts.

I looked up and smiled at him. I knew Maurice wanted me to be more than a friend to him. Even before I met Xavier, I wasn't feeling Maurice. When we were around and out with each other, we were never able to connect like that. I was already leaning forward.

He was standing too close in front of me. It looked like I was about to give him head. I sat up quickly and shook my head no. I didn't want Xavier to turn this bitch out.

"No, I'm good Maurice. Why don't you ask Tori?" I suggested.

"Hell no. You know Tori can't do nothing but shake her ass. She doesn't know how to two-step the way Tee Robin showed us. Come on P, just one dance." He begged.

"Maybe next time." Xavier's voice came from behind Maurice.

"I don't think that it is your place to answer for her." Maurice replied to Xavier, but his eyes were still on mine. I jumped up and went to Xavier.

"It is his place Maurice. This is my fiancée, Xavier. Xavier, this is Jessica's cousin Maurice." I quickly made the introductions. Maurice was shocked. He stared at me with hurt and confusion. I felt the rumble in Xavier's chest building up. I grabbed Xavier's hand to calm him down.

Maurice snapped out of his trance and finally spoke. "If she is your fiancée, you need to put a ring on her finger. Patience is one helluva catch. You don't want to lose her to some misunderstanding." Maurice replied with a smirk on his face.

Xavier showed off that beautiful smile and took a step forward. "She doesn't need a ring on her finger to know who she belongs to. And you know who she's for without it. It's up to you to respect it or not. Should I explain the consequences of the 'or not' part." Xavier told him, without the growl or his wolf appearing. He was showing his Alpha side through the man that he had always been.

Maurice took a step back and walked towards the rest of Jessica's family. Xavier lifted my hand and kissed my open palm. He turned and walked back to where my brothers were. Maxi and Xavion stupid asses were holding their stomachs laughing. I couldn't stand them at times. Nico and Ms. Robin were dancing. It was so surprising to see that she was his mate. It looked like they were going to have to tell Jeff sooner than later.

"Are you ok, Angel?" Papi came up from behind and asked me.

"Yeah, I'm ok." I said unsure.

"You want to talk about it." He said, walking in front of me and taking my hands in his. He started swaying from side to side. I couldn't do nothing but smile and fall in step. "I don't know Papi. How am I supposed to control Chaos, when she doesn't want to be controlled? She wants to be free and do whatever she wants." I told him the truth.

"You have to talk to her, Angel. You can't just shut her out like she doesn't exist. She is a part of you, whether you like it or not. The sooner you recognize that, the more control you will have over your power. She has a lot of information about you stored. For you to get that, you have to show her that you are ready to accept her." Papi said. He was making a lot of sense.

"Can you help me with that?" I asked him. I knew I couldn't do this alone.

"Yes, Angel. You are the reason why I am here." He told me. I could feel eyes burning in the back of my head. I heard Papi and Xavier's conversation. I didn't want to have to play referee to them every day. I needed them to get along. They were amongst the most important men in my life.

"Papi, what is up with you and Xavier." I came out and asked.

"I don't think he is right for you Angel. He won't be able to protect you like a strong Guardian could." He stopped dancing and stared me in the eyes. "You are all I have left. I don't want to put you in the hands of a man that isn't worthy. Besides that, you don't know each other. All this mating and fate shit feels rushed."

"It's not rushed, Papi." I replied. "I have known Xavier since he was a boy."

"But you don't know him as a man, Angel. People change. They develop bad habits that could harm you in the long run." He snapped.

"Papi it's different." I placed my hand on his chest to calm him. "I can say the same about you. I don't know if your intentions are good or not. But I let you in, despite all the stories I heard about you. My relationship with Xavier is different from the relationships of the Guardians. My wolf connects with him. When we mate with each other, I will see everything that has happened in his life. He will see the same from me." I placed my hand on his cheek and continued talking. "He is what I need, Papi. If you feel that he can't protect me, show him how to get around the magic that threatens me." I said sincerely.

Papi looked down at me with love in his eyes. "You are so young Angel, but very wise. If this is who you need, I will do my best to prepare him and you to survive this shit." He answered and started dancing with me again. When the song was over, he picked me up in a tight hug and placed me back on my feet. "Xavier," he yelled. Xavier walked over to me. Papi placed my hand into Xavier's. "Don't fuck up," he told him, before walking off.

Xavier shook his head and pulled my body into his. "I guess that's him going easy on me." He asked.

"Yeah, I guess so." I answered. He wrapped those big ass arms around my waist. He placed his face into my neck and moaned. The smell that only can be described as Xavier, teased all my senses. His soft lips pressed on my sweet spot. I wrapped my arms around him and pulled him closer. "Xavier," I moaned out. He pulled back and looked down at me.

"Time still," he asked. I wanted to tell him, fuck time. But, there were other things that needed to be handed.

"Time," I confirmed. He nodded his head and we continued dancing.

I woke up the next day without the pain or any new bruises. I knew it had something to do with Chaos not making an appearance. I got up and went to the bathroom to perform my morning ritual. After that, I went into the kitchen to start breakfast. Xavier was about to get up to go to work. I wanted to make him breakfast this time. I pulled out some grits, eggs, bacon, sausage, potatoes, and cheese.

I took out all the pots and pans that I needed to prepare breakfast. I told Papi to come by early, so that we can get started with my training. I was fixing plates when Xavier came down. He was dressed in his Sheriff's uniform. His dreads were still fresh from last night, but he took it out of the bun. They were in a low ponytail, with a thick string holding them in place.

"I could have done that Queen." Xavier said. He walked behind me and leaned forward to kiss me on my cheek. "Good morning."

"Good morning. And it's ok. I don't mind cooking for you, Xavier." I told him. I walked around the island to create space between the two us. He smiled and shook his head at my action. But I do love the fact that he was respecting me. "What is on your agenda today?" I asked.

"Work and more work. We got a contract to build a building in the city. Xavion and I will meet up with the clients to get the specifics. I will also get with Dom and the rest of your brothers later. We were thinking of building a new school and hospital. After that, I'll be on my way home to you." He said. I passed him his plate and prepared another for Papi. "What are your plans?'

"I will be training with Papi. Nico taught me everything that I need to know about my wolf, while you were away. There are other things that I need to learn but that is going to have to wait. I need to get Chaos under control." I told him.

"Queen, tell me about your nightmares, baby." He asked while eating his food. That was a subject that I didn't want to talk about at the time. I didn't want to relive that shit again. I finally was able to keep the nightmares away. But, I couldn't ignore what I have seen with my own eyes, when I woke up. "Can we talk about that later, please?" I asked.

"Ok. Whenever you ready to, let me know. I am here." He said with so much understanding. Papi knocked before walking in the back door.

"You ready, Angel. We gotta get to work." He said without speaking.

"Morning, Papi. How did you sleep?" I greeted.

He looked at me and let out a deep breath. "Good morning, Angel." He said with a smile. He nodded his head at Xavier and Xavier did the same. It was a work in progress, I guess. Papi grabbed his plate of food and walked back out the door.

"I'll see you later," I told Xavier. I was walking out the back door, when he stopped me.

"I know you need time and all, Queen. But, I don't ever want you to think that it is ok for you to walk out this house without kissing or hugging me." He told me with a low growl. I turned and walked back towards him. He turned in his seat and spread his legs for me to stand in between them. I leaned in and gave him a soft kiss on his lips. Xavier grabbed me and held me where I stood. "Don't let that happen again. Understand." He demanded. I nodded my head and made a quick exit out the back door.

Papi was standing by one of the trees in our yard. "Do you want to start here, or do you want to go further in?" he asked. I looked around and saw that I might need more space. "Let's go further in." I answered and flipped over the gate that was blocking the wind from coming in. Papi followed, after placing his empty plate on the back porch.

When we got further in, he began to tell me what to do. "How do you call to your wolf?" He asked.

"I see her in my head. I connect with her to let her know when she can come out." I answered. He nodded his head, as if that was the answer he was looking for.

"Good. Now, see your black magic. Feel it flow through your veins. And let it out piece by piece. Don't feed into the rage and the hate. That is what she needs to survive. Give her an inch." Papi told me.

I reached inside of myself to try to connect with her. I saw my wolf stepping forward, not wanting her to get loose. I concentrated harder and I saw her standing over all of those Guardians at the Southern Facility. Her back is turned towards me. I walked up slowly behind her to get her attention. She turned to me quickly and grabbed me by my neck.

"You can't keep me in here forever." She said to me with her wolf teeth and red eyes. She swiped her claws down my face and I woke up. Papi and Nico were standing over me. I stood and felt something running down my face. It was blood. This bitch clawed my face up.

"She is angry, Angel. You can't bottle up that type of magic. You gotta let it go sometimes or it's going to kill you." Papi said.

"Fuck letting her out. Do you see what that bitch did to my face?" I yelled. I was more than mad.

"Tell us what you saw." Nico asked. I looked up at him and laid back down on the ground.

"I saw her standing over the Guardians' bodies. I walked up to her and she grabbed me by my throat. She had wolf teeth and claws with red eyes." I replied.

"Oh, shit. She relates to your rogue wolf." Nico said.

"What does that mean for me?" I asked.

"That means you have a lot of work to do." Papi answered.

SEVENTEEN

Xavier

I was at the Sheriff's station going over a couple of complaints. One of the members of our pack saw some hunters on our land. I was going to have to go to St. Charles Police Department. I was cool with the Captain over there. I already told him that if we caught anyone hunting on our property that we won't be responsible for any wild animal attacks. He agreed and set the law in motion. They always had a few of them, that didn't think that the law applied to them. I had to let Dom know about this complaint, so that they can keep a close eye on their property as well.

I looked down at my watch and saw that it was almost time for me to attend that meeting with the clients. Xander and Xavion walked into my office. Xavion closed the door while Xander sat in the chair in front my desk. I sat back and waited for them to speak their mind. "What can we do to help with you and Queen?" Xander asked.

"What are you doing back so early?" I told him. I thought he would have been under Jess for a week, at least.

"I'm not back. I'm giving her some time to rest and heal." He said. I looked up to Xavion, waiting for him to say something slick. He didn't disappoint, when his mouth opened to reply.

"Stop lying. Yo ass was howling all night fool. You the one that needed the break. Don't blame that shit on my sister-in-law." He said before mushing Xander's head.

"Shut the fuck up. You are sitting here talking about how I was howling through the night, but Loreen had yo ass embarrassing yourself at the ceremony." He replied.

That shut Xavion up. He went and sat in the chair by the window. "What's up with that? Do you think that she is your mate?" I asked. He shook his head no.

"I feel something with her; it's just not as strong as the mating pull. I do get pissed off when someone approaches her or when she gives another man attention." He sighed, like he was going through something that we didn't know about.

"Von, what's up bruh?" I asked him.

"I don't know, X. Ever since the battle between us and the Guardians, something has been off. I don't know what it is, but I feel it." He said looking out of the window. The phone began to ring, interrupting our conversation.

I picked it up and answered, "Sheriff King."

"Yes, is this Xavier King." The woman said on the other end.

"This is he," I answered.

"Hi, Xavier. I am Elizabeth Vandis, your grandmother." She said. I placed her on speaker, so that my brothers could hear the conversation.

"My grandmother." I said, letting my brothers know who I was talking to. They both came scooting up closer to the desk.

"What can I do for your Mrs. Vandis." I asked her. I wasn't calling her grandma or anything near it. They fucked over my mother. I wasn't showing respect to any of them.

"Well, I was wondering if we can come and see you. Your father didn't really want us around before. We thought that if you were older you may have wanted to get to know the rest of your family. I am calling to see if it is ok if we can come and meet you." She answered.

"You do know that you have other grandchildren." I told her.

"Oh yes, the other X boys. How are they?" She replied. Xavion and Xander chuckled at the fact that she didn't know their names.

"They are fine, Mrs. Vandis. I would like to know why you want to visit me, all of a sudden."

"I think that we need to discuss this in person. It will be me and your grandfather. We will be there in two days. See you soon." She said and hung up the phone.

"What the hell was that all about?" Xavion asked.

"I don't know, but I do know that we have to tell mom that her parents are coming to visit me and the X boys." I said standing up.

"Wait, Xavier. What are you going to do about Queen?" Xander asked.

I picked the phone up and dialed Nick's number.

"What's up?" He answered.

"Can you send Maxi over to meet with some clients with Xavion? I got a call from my mother's parents. They are coming to visit in two days. I got to tell my mom and make sure Chaos doesn't make an appearance at the meeting." I told him.

"That's cool. Let me know the place that you are meeting them, so that I can keep Lil Bit away." He told me. He already knew what I needed him to do.

"Thanks, brother. I'll call you when I get the other details." I told him and hung up.

"Are you going to tell Queen about the meeting." Xavion asked. "I don't want her beating your ass in front of your grandparents." Xavion joked.

"After I tell mom, I will go home and talk to her about it. We promised each other that we won't be holding back any secrets." I answered and walked out of the office. There were a lot of shifters hanging around not doing much. Errol was at the front desk going over paperwork. "Hey watch the fort. If you need anything, call me or Xavion. Xander will be out for the remainder of the week."

"No problem, Alpha." He answered. They usually answered me that way when there was no one else around. I turned to Xander and Xavion. "Xander, stay yo ass away from this station and tell Jess don't worry about Queen. I got this under control. Xavion, after I talked to Queen and Mom, me and you will talk about whatever it is that you are feeling. We can't help you, bruh, if you don't tell us that there is a problem." I told them and jumped in my truck. I didn't know what my mother was going to say about this shit. She already moved on from their decision. I hoped they knew that I was more like my father.

I pulled up to my mother's home and she was sitting on the swing with Ms. Robin. We found out that Ms. Robin was Nico's mate. He been all over Ms. Robin. She been giving him hell though. She was old school for sure. She told him that they won't be rushing to get mated. She had to get to know him as a man first. Nico didn't object. He felt that he had been waiting this long, a couple more weeks couldn't hurt.

I walked up the stairs and greeted the women. "Hello, ladies."

"Why are you here? Shouldn't you be home trying to get Queen to mate with you?" Mom said while rolling her eyes. She was big mad at me. You would have thought that Queen was her daughter.

"I am on my way over there after this, Ma." I told her.

"I received a call today. It was Elizabeth Vandis. She wanted to come and visit with Grandfather." I told her. My mom looked up and I swear I thought I saw her eyes shift.

"When are they coming?" She said with a scheming smile.

I shook my head and answered. "In two days. I don't know where yet."

"I do. Let them bring their asses here." She said. I didn't know what my mom had up her sleeve. But if this was where she wanted to have it, that was fine by me. I didn't want to have it too close to where Queen was going to be. Dom stayed at least fifty miles from my mother's house. I was going to see if he would take her into the city.

"Alright, Ma." I told her and turned to go home. I can hear her telling Ms. Robin about her parents. I was happy that she had someone else to talk to. Loreen, Tori, and Jess were rubbing off on her. Every now and then she would say that something was ratchet or that she wanted to get lit at the ceremony. The girls found the shit funny, but me and my brothers weren't feeling this shit.

When I got home, Queen was still training with her grandfather. You could hear her grandfather's voice from the front of the road. I got out and followed the voices to the back of the house.

"Angel, give her a little more room, baby." Matteo said. When I got into their sight, Queen had blood running down her face. Her eyes were flashing red, white, then hazel. I was about to step in, but Nico motioned for me to stay where I was.

I stopped and stood still. It was hard to see her like this. Her body was covered with sweat. I felt her wolf calling out for help and it was killing me. Matteo saw that she was about to go over. He told her to relax and that they will continue their training on tomorrow. I walked up behind her and pulled her into a hug. She sighed.

"Thank you." She told me.

"Why are you thanking me, Queen?" I asked her. She turned around to face me. Her wounds were healing in front my eyes.

"Thank you for being here. Something inside you called out to me. It wasn't your wolf or your Guardian side. It was you." She told me. I was hoping that, that would have been the end of our disagreement.

"Alright, boy. It's your turn. Angel, you go wash up and get some rest. We will have dinner ready for you when you wake up." He told her. I looked back into her eyes and saw how tired she was. They have been going at it for five hours nonstop. I was confused, though.

"What am I training for?" I asked him. Queen put her head on my shoulder and waited for Matteo to answer.

He let out a deep breath before he started talking. You can tell he was being forced to do this. "If you are going to be with my granddaughter, you will have to know the ins and outs of the Guardian magic. You told Angel that she is rejecting Chaos, but you are also rejecting your Guardian side. I will show you how to connect with your other side, so that you won't have to keep fucking Chaos." He answered. He knew that he didn't have to say that last part. He was taking jabs and adding salt to an open wound.

"Be nice, Papi." Queen said, unbothered by the shit that came out of his mouth. "You behave as well. I need you both to get along. Whether any of you like it or not, you guys will be the key of my outcome." She told us both. She gave me the sweetest kiss on my lips. She turned and walked back to the house with Nico following her. I turned to face Matteo. His eyes were dark and cold.

"I need you to call on your Guardian side." He told me like that shit was simple.

"I don't know how to do that. It comes out when I need it or when I am angry about something. I can't will it out just because." I told him.

"You can feel it. It's the opposite feeling of your wolf. Your wolf is always on the edge, ready to attack at any time. Your mental powers are calm." He said.

"That is not true. When I was fighting the Alphas that challenged me for Queen, I was able to hit them with shockwaves that killed them." I told him. I wasn't going to hold nothing back. I was willing to do anything to protect my Queen. "I was also able to teleport from one place to another. Not as far as the other Guardians, but three miles is the max. And when Aunt Lurita called out to my magic when we were at the station, something else called out to me. It had me in pure rage when Aunt Lurita took Queen out the room. Is that still considered being a Mental?" I asked.

He smiled and shook his head. "Yes, you are a Mental. A whole one. She increased your power. Guardians feed off the energy and magic of other Guardians." He walked closer to me. He was debating on telling me what he was thinking.

"I know you don't think that I am good enough for Queen. But if there is something that I need to know to protect, you better tell me. I can't protect her from something, if I don't know what that something is." I told him.

He stared into my eyes. He wanted to know if I could be trusted. He let out another breath and nodded his head. "I already told you that Chaos went to the Southern Guardian Facility. She killed everyone there and burned the facility down. When I got there, some of the bodies were mauled and gnawed. Chaos has bounded with Angel's wolf. Her wolf was in dark form. Rogue. The rogue wolf and Chaos murdered and destroyed a facility within fifteen minutes. Chaos has got information from one of the Supremes that was over the facility. Angel will have to communicate with Chaos to get the information that we need, to find out who ordered the hit on her parents." He finished.

I couldn't believe the shit that I was hearing. They were going to come after her. The Guardians were going to attack her with everything that they had. Not only did I have to prepare myself, but my brothers and the pack as well. I also had to let Nick know. "You didn't describe the way the Guardians were killed before. Why wait and tell me this shit now?" I asked him angrily. "Do she remember anything?" I asked him.

"She doesn't remember what Chaos did, but she did see the aftermath of it all." Matteo answered.

"Fuck," I yelled out. "When we found her, she was crying and feeling some type of way about something. We just thought that it was the death of Aunt Lurita." I started pacing back and forth. She was probably thinking that she was a monster, if waking up to that scene. I got to get stronger for her. If I gotta be that fucking monster, I'll be that. I don't want that shit over her head. She was a gift. My gift. I didn't want her to think of herself as anything else. I stopped and looked at Matteo. With nothing but determination, I told him, "Let's get to work."

EIGHTEEN

Patience

$\mathcal{I}$t's been three days and I have been learning everything piece by piece. After I finished training, Xavier came to train after me. It seemed like he had been working harder than usual. When he came in, he would eat, then go into the guest bedroom. I craved his touch in the worst way. Chaos and the wolf have been calling out to him. She was never going to get him that way again. If I couldn't be present for their rendezvous, she wasn't going to come through at all.

When we were training, she came through with so much rage. Nico was trying to distract her, so that Papi could push her back. She sent him flying through the woods. He didn't have control over her anymore. It was different from the other times. I was sitting in the front seat of my mind watching everything play out. When she was about to attack Papi again, I pulled her back and reclaimed my body and was back to myself.

"You did it." He told me as he gasped for air. I told him the difference and he said that I was becoming stronger.

I was in my room after that intense training. I wanted to go in Xavier's room, but he looked more tired than me. I wasn't looking for him to make love to me. I just needed him to hold me. I knew that he was trying to help control Chaos. I just wished that he would have talked to me about it. I closed my eyes and tried to go to sleep, but I couldn't, not without him. I got up and walked out our bedroom. Xavier was sleeping in the room across from ours. He said that he wanted to be close to me. I walked to the door and knocked. I didn't get an answer. I turned the doorknob and it was unlocked. I went into the room and saw my Alpha sleeping on the right side of the bed. The covers were pulled down to his waist. I knew that he was naked underneath. That was the only way he slept. Like I said before, I wasn't here for sex.

I walked towards the left side of the bed and climbed in. Xavier turned his body towards mine. He wrapped his arm around my waist and pulled me closer to his body.

"I love you, Queen." He said in a groggy voice.

"I love you, Alpha." I told him and in no time, I fell asleep.

I was back at the Guardian facility. I saw Chaos taking out all of the men. She was sucking his energy out of his body. After that was done, she opened her mouth and bit the Guardian in the face. I turned away and waited until she was done. When I looked back at her, she was staring at me. I maintained eye contact and walked towards her.

"So, little Patience came to play with me." She said with red eyes and her wolf was present. Her mouth was dripping with blood.

"I didn't come to play with you Chaos. I just need to know something. What is it that you want from me?" I asked. She snapped her teeth in me. I knew that she wasn't trying to scare me. I already owed her ass for scratching me in the face.

"I want to be free! I am tired of getting stuck in here. If you will let me out, I wouldn't let you relive this part of your life. I knew that you would feel some type of way because I acted out what you thought about doing." She snarled.

"You want out!" I yelled, taking a few steps forward. "Why? So, you can run around and do this. You didn't think about the repercussions of your actions. Our actions. Guardians are going to come at me and our family because of this shit." I spat out. "You have to understand that things can't be worked out this way."

"You are so weak. No wonder Xavier loves me more." She replied.

I lost it after that. My hair grew longer in gold. My claws came out, but my

118

wolf teeth weren't present. I threw a strong gust of wind at her, knocking her a few yards back.

"You will stay away from him." I said in a chiming voice. She recovered quickly and through a black mass at me. When it got close to me, I smacked it to one of the trees to my left. She countered with another ball. I couldn't prepare for that one and it hit me in the chest. It knocked me back and left a stinging sensation on my skin. I got up and she was swinging at me with her claws out. I dodged them and hit her with an electric shock. She snarled back and transformed all the way to the rogue wolf. It came at me full force. I dug my feet into the ground and grabbed her snapping snout. She growled and shook her head left to right.

"I didn't come here to fight you, Chaos. Despite what you think, you need me, just like I need you." I told her still holding on. How could I talk to her, when she was ready to kill me? I threw her wolf and changed back to my regular self. "I came here to call a truce." I told her. She got up and transformed back into the Guardian.

"How do I know that you can be trusted?" She asked.

"How do I know that you can be trusted?" I replied instead. I looked around, emphasizing what she has done when she was in control. She looked around and saw my meaning. She pulled her wolf back in.

"This was something that you wanted to do, Patience. I act out your deepest, darkest desires." She told me. I walked up to her with my hands up, surrendering to all this bullshit.

"I get that, but this wasn't the way I wanted to do this. I can promise you that we will get those who set Mom and Daddy up. I want to be there with you making those decisions though, Chaos. I want to remember what was done and know that it was a mutual decision on both ends. And when people come to retaliate, for what we did, I can be aware and be on guard. Don't leave me in the dark."

It looked like I was making progress. Her red eyes were still glaring at me. I stood and waited for her to make the next move. She knew that her decision was going to make us or break us.

"I need to show you something." She said. She reached out her hand to me. I looked down at it and wondered if I can really trust her. I needed to, if I wanted her to trust me. I placed my hand into hers, and she teleported us to the tree that I escaped to. It stood strong from the root, all the way to the tip of the branches.

"You always wonder why you couldn't feel Daddy. When Mom passed away, Aunt Lurita wanted you to know Mom but not Dad. She didn't want you to know about your wolf half because she didn't want you to suffer like Mom did. So, she took Mom's ashes and brought them with her. She spread them in Texas, so that we can feel at home. She wasn't counting on the other empty part of us to come through the way it did. She tried to fill it with other shit, but we needed our father. You always wonder why this trail." She said and placed her hand on the tree. *"It was because he was calling out to you. After Mom died, I burned Daddy's ashes and spread them here. This tree is the center. This is where his energy is."* She told me.

I looked up at the tree and felt it calling out to me. I placed my hand on it and felt the strength and the love of my father. I couldn't understand how it comforted me the other day. I knew now. I felt the tears run down my face.

"Daddy," I asked. The branches began to move and circled around me. I couldn't believe it. I closed my eyes and a vision came to me.

"Lil Bit, what are you doing out here? It is late, and you need to be in the bed." Daddy said, walking from his truck and onto the porch where I was sitting. I was looking at the stars that filled the dark sky with so much light.

"Look, Daddy. Don't that look like your boot?" I told him. He sat next to me and looked up.

"Yeah, it actually does." He said with a chuckle. *"But you didn't answer me, why are you up?"*

"I couldn't sleep. Maxi was snoring loudly. I didn't want to turn on the television and wake everyone, so I decided to come out here and look at the sky. It's beautiful out here." I told him. We sat in silence and stared up at the stars.

"You know if your Mom caught you out here, you'll get in trouble." Daddy said.

"No, I won't. As long as I have you here with me, Mom won't say anything." I replied. I could feel his smile growing on his face. When the stars no longer held my attention, I looked at my Daddy, who was staring down at me. *"Why are you looking at me like that?"* I asked him. He smiled at me again before answering.

"The world can be so cruel at times. I face the ugliness of it every day. But, when I come home to your mother, my sons, and you, everything becomes clear. I wouldn't change none of the bad things that have happened to me, if it would lead me to you guys." He said to me.

He was worried about something. He wasn't going to tell me what, because I was only a child. Even if I could help, he would always keep whatever to his self. I gave him some of my energy and felt the tension leave his body. He pulled back and shook his head.

"Lil Bit, you didn't have to do that. Keep your energy baby girl. Daddy didn't need it." He told me now without the tiredness in his eyes.

"I know Daddy." I told him. He smiled down at me and stood with me in his arms. Every time I transfer energy to any of my brothers, I became tired, weak even. This was no different. I felt sleepy and was ready to sleep through Maxi's snoring. Daddy put me into bed and gave me a kiss goodnight.

"I'll tell your mother to give you a couple more hours to sleep." He said.

"Ok, Daddy. I love you."

"I love you more." He told me. I lifted my head and beamed at him. "Not today." I said and went to sleep with no problems.

When I woke up, I was in the bed with Xavier's arms wrapped around me. I had tears coming down my face.

"Daddy," I whispered. My Daddy was here the whole time. I had to tell my brothers. I was getting out of the bed, when a strong arm reached out and pulled me back in. He tucked under him and held on tightly.

"Where are you going, Queen? It is three in the morning." He said tiredly. I looked over at the clock and it was three. I didn't know how long I slept but it felt like forever. I closed my eyes and Chaos was there. She smiled at me and nodded her head.

"Thank you," I told her.

"What are you thanking me for Queen?" Xavier asked. I didn't know that I said it out loud. I cuddled back into my Alpha.

～

The next morning, I woke up with so much on my mind. I got up and cooked breakfast for Papi and Xavier. Ms. Robin was leaving today to go back to Texas. She was going to put her two weeks' notice in and transfer Jeff down here for school. Papi told Nico that he could have gone with her, because I had all the protection I needed. Xavier came down the stairs on his phone.

"Alright, I'll be right there." He said and hung up his phone. "Hey Queen." He said and pulled me into a hug. "What was going on with you last night." He asked.

Papi walked in the before I could answer. "Good, now I don't have to worry about saying this twice." I told them. I fixed them plates and they both sat down. I placed their plates in front of them and remembered Xavier's phone conversation. "Xavier, do you need to go?" I asked him.

He shook his head. "You are more important. What is it Queen?" He said and pushed his plate aside. I loved him more when he was like that. His eyes were on mine and he was waiting to protect me from whatever.

"I talked to Chaos last night." I stated. Xavier's eyes went wide. Papi stopped eating and stared at me.

"And," he replied.

"We fought a little bit, but in the end, we came to an agreement. If I was to let her be free, she would behave with me still there. I asked her if she can be trusted, in good faith, she showed me something." I said.

I felt the tears coming and Xavier felt my mood change. He stood and came to me. "What did she show you, Queen? Talk to us, baby." He asked in that soothing voice. I leaned into his body for the support that he was giving me. My Alpha wrapped his arm around me and gave me whatever I needed. I took a deep breath before continuing.

"She showed me where my father rests." I told them in a whisper. Xavier didn't know what to say. Papi was still stunned from my interaction with her. They gave me some time to recover before asking me the question that I didn't get the answer to.

"Did she tell you what she found out at the Guardian Facility?" Papi asked. I shook my head no. "But, I can let her out, and you can ask her yourself." I suggested.

"Can we go outside? I need to be in the open for this." I told them. They both nodded their heads. Xavier kissed me on my lips and grabbed my hand.

"I am going to be right here Queen, no matter what." He said before walking me to the back door with Papi following.

When I got to the last step, I dropped Xavier's hand and went to the middle of the yard. I closed my eyes and concentrated on us. Concentrated on the bond that we needed to have to survive in one body. "Chaos," I called out. Chaos came forward with a smile.

"Trust me sis," She said to me. I nodded my head and let her through.

Chaos

It feels good to be out. She really trusted me. I didn't want to disappoint her. I turned around and saw my Alpha standing next to another. He was the one that pushed me back in when I came out a few times. I didn't know if they were toying with me or trying to put me to sleep. When Patience told me that we needed to work together, at first, I thought it was a trick. But when she stopped fighting me, I knew that she was looking for a truce. The man before me was different from my Xavier. His soul was dark. I could see the dark power running through him. It was toxic. I called out to his dark power and saw the demon that lurked inside him. It ran free in his mind and was under control. Unlike me, I was caged in a box, in Patience's mind. His dark magic came forth. The man before me stepped forward with black eyes.

"Queen," He said before kneeling.

"Grandfather." I responded by nodding my head.

I was happy that he caught on to who I truly was. If he didn't, he would have never survived a small attack from me. He got up and continued talking.

"Queen, we need to know what happened at the Southern Guardian Facility." He asked. Patience told me that, that was something that she needed to know to protect her family. Our family. I looked over to my Alpha and motioned him to come closer. He walked towards me with power in each stride. I saw my dark power in him, but not as much. When he was standing next to my grandfather, I held out my hand for them to grab. Grandfather did it without hesitation. You could see that Alpha was questioning it.

"I won't bite Alpha, unless Patience gives me the permission to." I told him. He still didn't believe what I was saying. So, I let Patience come through to show him that this was her idea. I closed my eyes and opened again. He saw his Queen in my eyes. He nodded his head and placed his hand in mine.

I teleported us back to the Southern Guardian Facility. The Guardians cleaned up the place and started rebuilding it. I knew that they were going to do this. I didn't mind destroying it all over again. I waved my hand and the scene before us got blurry. Everything was going backwards. When it came to a stop, we were brought back to the day I destroyed it. We saw when I appeared out of nowhere. I stepped forward and merged with my body. I looked back and motioned for Xavier and my grandfather to follow me all the way through. I wanted to relive this moment as much as I could.

They witnessed how I burned the Guardian's guards on the outside. When I went in and saw the rest of the Guardian's guards there, I didn't waste time with them either. None of them had the information I needed. One of the guards threw some weak magic at me. I blocked it and sent acid down all of their throats. I felt the wolf wanting to play with me, so I let her out, on my terms. She gave me her claws and teeth. The next guard that approached me, got snatched and bitten. I was feeding off their energy and the wolf was feeding off their flesh.

There were more dark Guardians present, but they didn't have shit on me. I didn't want them to interrupt shit that I was doing. The wolf bit the face of one Guardian and spat it at the other. I turned around and looked past the men that were following me, but into the woods. I pulled the wolf back and winked in that direction. I turned and continued walking through the facility with poison in my touch. I held my hands up and everything melted when I touched it. I blew fire in all of the rooms I passed. When I got to my destination, the door was locked shut with ten more guards with the assassin symbol on their heads.

They didn't know how to react because I was something that none of them knew about. Of course, they knew Patience was a mixture of a wolf and a Guardian. But no one knew about me. Chaos.

"Is the Supreme you're protecting worth more than your life." I asked them all. When they didn't answer, I assumed that they didn't want to talk to me, which was rude. "Oh, well. You can't say I didn't let you try and talk your way out of it." I told them.

The guards started throwing masses of electric balls at me. I was batting that shit away with ease. "Whoever was the trainer of this weak magic, need their ass whipped." I mumbled before taking them all out by cutting off their air supply. I pushed the assassin out of the way as he tried to gasp for the air that wasn't there. I pulled the door open and the Supreme Guardian was sitting behind his desk. He thought that no one would get past his assassins. I felt insulted.

"Who are you?" He asked.

"You don't know who I am?" I asked him sarcastically. "Let us not play these games, Latimore. You know who I am and why I am here. We can do this the hard way or the harder way. You choose but be mindful. A lot of your Guardians didn't have this choice." I growled. I let the wolf claws come through my fingers. His eyes got wider. "Ahhhh, you didn't think that I had control over the wolf. Well I have control and she wants to come out and play."

He recovered from his shock and tried to boss up on me. "You cannot be here. Your kind isn't welcome. Get out of my facility before I remove you from it." He said with his eyes changing into a lavender color. I started laughing at him. Clearly, he didn't know that there was no facility left. His office was the last room left. "Do you find something funny, you half-breed?" He spat.

I stopped laughing after that. I didn't like being called that, neither did Patience. I knew that we would have agreed to killing him slowly. But, I did have to let him know who I was. My claws came all the way out. My skin became dull and cold. My eyes were already red, but they were brighter. My inky black hair grew along with my teeth.

His skin got ashy and his mouth dropped open. Sweat was running down his face and his body was shaking with fear. "Now, Latimore, you and I know that I am more than a half-breed. I am the Queen of the Darkness. I am what you Supremes fear. You knew what I was and what I would become. You sent those assassins to my home and took the loves of our lives." I told him in a dark voice. I walked towards a stunned Latimore. He couldn't move, and it wasn't my magic that was stopping him. I got in front of him and saw the reflection of myself in his eyes. I smiled and then grabbed his chin. I stared into his eyes and went into his mind.

There were six Supremes sitting around the table with another man. He stood strong and had so much power. A picture of me and my parents were sitting on the table. "The board has agreed along with the rest of the Alphas on the board. Send out the assassins and kill the child. She will be a major threat to us and the wolves. We can't go through with any type of exposure. If Nesida or the wolf can't control her, she will risk us all. Send out the first wave. If they survive that, send on the next and the next, until the three of them are dead. We will let the other Alphas know when this is done so that they can go after the wolve's land and property." One of the oldest Supremes said. They were all in some white cloaks. The man that stood with them was dressed in a black cloak with the assassin symbol on it. He didn't have the sign on his head like the rest of them. "I will go with the group and make sure that it is done." He spoke out.

A younger Supreme stood and said something totally different. "Maybe we can bring the child here. We all can feed off her energy and become more power-ful. We can then get rid of the Dark Lord for good." He suggested.

"No, we don't want to tamper with that type of magic Tarrine. This thing is not something that I want around too long." Another older Guardian said.

The man they called Tarrine sat and was disappointed. He looked like he had something up his sleeves. I had to find him as soon as possible. "We shall vote on the matter." Another Supreme spoke. "All in favor of killing this off this half-breed, light your candle." Latimore was the first along with the other four. Tarrine didn't light his candle. "Majority rules. Send now in the order that was

discussed. We don't want to hear of this matter again," The oldest one spoke
again."

I saw what I needed to see. His ass couldn't wait for them to kill
my family. I wanted the other one that went with the assassins to
make sure the job was done. "Thank you so much for the information. You, unlike the rest of them, was truly helpful. Now, did you
have time to choose." I asked a now older Supreme. I was draining
his life's energy while I was looking into his mind. He didn't look
like he could stand up much longer. "Well, Latimore. Since you
inflict pain on us so readily. Let's see you inflict that pain on yourself." I told him.

I placed my finger on his forehead and placed a demon into
him. When I removed my finger, his pale lavender eyes went black.
He looked at me and smiled. "Hello, my child, do what you must."
He nodded happily and took a hefty bite of his arm. He spat the
piece out and began tearing his own body up. I sat in the chair and
watched.

When he was done, I took the remaining energy. I knew what
my next destination was going to be. I just had to get loose, so that I
can get started on my next trip. I turned around towards Alpha and
Grandfather. They were looking at me like something was wrong
with me. I let out a deep breath and tried to stay calm. Patience was
chanting that in my head.

"Thank you, Queen. Can I please talk to my Angel? We need to
discuss a couple of things with her. We will be seeing you soon."
Grandfather asked.

I wanted to see my mother and aunt again. I popped up when
Patience was mad and saw them from time to time. I missed them
just like Patience did. I stepped forward and looked into his mind.
There I saw a young version of my mother and aunt. I saw them
playing with each other and then battling each other. He tried to
help but Aunt Lurita didn't want a truce between them. I saw him
surrendering to them and the way they kept him in the box. I
stepped back and looked into his eyes. "Thank you for helping
Patience connect with me." I told him. I turned towards Alpha with
a smirk. "We have plans for you." I said with a chuckle.

NINETEEN

Xavier

---

*N*ow that we knew what happened at the Guardian Facility, it was time to start setting up our own guards around our territories. I was headed to my mother's house to meet up with the Vandis. I told Queen about it and she didn't want to attend. She went to help Cam and Treasure at the hospital. I called Dom and told him that we had to meet up about what Chaos showed us. I pulled up and saw that Xavion was already here. I told his ass to come by the house so that we could talk. I was gon' fuck him up.

He had to understand that we couldn't help him, if he doesn't tell us the problem. I knew that he was avoiding the conversation, but it had to happen. I walked into the house and my mom had everything laid out for the guests. I shook my head, when I saw the picture of my father in wolf form, placed on the opposite wall of where the guest would be sitting. She wanted them to feel his presence. And how his wolf was staring out with a menacing growl, they were going to be uncomfortable.

I walked to the kitchen and saw Xavion eating already. He was scrolling through his phone, when I slapped him on the back of his head. "Why weren't you at my house?" I asked.

"Look, Xavier, yo hands are heavy as fuck. Don't slap me like that." He said rubbing the back of his head.

"What's wrong with you, Von?" I asked and sat next to him. He let out a deep breath and his head dropped back. He looked worried and that bothered me. "I went to New Orleans one night when I was off a couple months ago with Maxi. We were looking for some girls to hook up with. Long story short, I met this girl named Eve. We had sex and after that she was talking about me being the one for her. I didn't think nothing of it, because that's how all the women reacted afterwards. I got up and was getting dressed. She asked me to meet her Grandmother Lozale. I dismissed her. She called out to me and I turned around. When I did, she blew some black shit in my face and told me that I was going to be hers forever. I didn't feel Guardian magic around her. It was something totally different.

In my heart, X, I know that Loreen is my mate. But whatever that bitch did to me that night, is fucking with my wolf. I love and hate Loreen. Last night when we were together, I couldn't make love to her the way I wanted. I fucked around and called out Eve's name because she was all I saw. Loreen got up and left. She hasn't been answering my texts or any of my calls. I am so fucked up X." He finished with his fist hitting the table.

I grabbed his fist and squeezed it to get his attention. He looked at me with so much sadness in his eyes. My brother was fucking hurting. I had an idea of what that bitch Eve was, but I wanted to make sure before I made any assumptions. "We are going to take care of this shit. Believe that. I will ask Queen to look into your head, so that she can get a visual of the chick. We will find her Von and reverse whatever she did to you. Ok." I told him.

"Yes, brother. Thank you." He said. He was relieved now that he got that off his chest. Xander walked in with hickeys all over his neck. He was sporting a silly ass grin on his face that made me and Xavion smile.

"What's up, brothers? Y'all grandparents didn't make it yet, I see." He said, jokingly. Xavion and I started laughing. Xavion shook his head and responded.

"That ain't my peoples. Don't play with me like that." He said still laughing.

"Oh yeah, my bad. That's Xavier's grandparents. We are just the other X boys." Xander said while making him a plate of food.

"Fuck both of y'all." I said and got up. I went to go look for my mom. I wanted to know how she was really feeling about her parents coming over. She was coming out of her bedroom, dressed in a pair of slacks and a red blouse. Red was my dad's favorite color. "You good with this Ma." I asked her. She looked up at me and smirked.

"Boy please. I have been waiting for this for a long time." She said and placed a kiss on my cheek.

I grabbed her hand and led her to the kitchen. Xavion and Xander were still clowning about the Vandis. When we walked in, they stopped and got up to kiss mom.

"Did you guys eat yet?" She asked.

"Yes ma'am," we all answered.

"Good," she answered. She began to bring some of the food out into the family room. After everything was set up, the doorbell rang.

Ma went to the door and opened it. The Vandis' were here, but they weren't alone. It looked like they brought another couple and a young woman with them.

"What the fuck are they doing here?" Ma asked. The older guy stepped forward and greeted Ma.

"We are doing fine, daughter. Thanks for asking." He said.

"I didn't because I don't give a fuck. You didn't say anything about bringing them here." Ma said pointing to the other people that were standing next to her parents. I stepped forward and stood next to my mother.

"Ma, it's ok. Come in." I told them while pulling my mother to the side. She was giving me the evil eye. "Don't worry about it, Ma. I got it under control." I told her. We stepped into the room and they were all staring at the picture of my father. Ma sat across from them with a wicked grin on her face. Xavion and Xander walked in and stood behind her with blank expressions on their faces.

"Please have a seat." I asked them. I let them sit first before I took my seat next to my mother.

"Thank you, son." Mr. Vandis said after taking his seat. "I'd like to introduce Catherine and Peter Patterson. And this is their daughter Daisy." He continued. Xavion and Xander chortled at her name. Mr. Vandis looked over my shoulder at the two. "And who may you two be." He asked.

Xavion smirked before saying, "Oh, us. Well, we are the other X boys."

"Xavion and Xander," I told them. "These are your other grandchildren."

"Oh, wow. You boys have grown to be large men." He replied.

"That's what they say," Xavion responded. Xander was trying to hold in his laugh but was losing that battle. My mother cleared her throat to get our attention. I could see that she was ready for them to get out of her house.

"Well, what brings you here?" Ma asked.

"We thought that Xavier would have liked to meet his future wife." Mrs. Vandis spoke for the first time. I didn't look over to the other woman. I turned my attention to Mr. Vandis.

"What was your last conversation with Nesida about?" I ignored Mrs. Vandis statement. Mr. Vandis looked at me in shock.

"I don't believe that you heard what your grandmother said. This is your future wife, son. She has been waiting to be with you her whole life." He said.

Mr. Patterson raised his hand to speak. "Hello, Xavier. My wife and I would like it if you could come by and we can discuss some things alone, with your mother of course."

"Yes, we would love to get to know your family better. Xavion and Xander are more than welcome to come. We do have many other single female Guardians looking for a strong healthy man to be with." Mrs. Patterson added. That shit wiped the smile of Xavion and Xander's face. Xander growled and stepped forward.

"I am already mated, ma'am. And I am pretty sure that Xavion will be soon. We don't need any of your single female Guardians." He growled.

Mr. Patterson started charging up his power to protect his wife from getting mauled by my brothers. I held my hand up for my brothers to stand down.

"I decline." I answered. "Now can we discuss the conversation you held with Nesida." I asked Mr. Vandis.

"Excuse me, your grandparents are right. When you marry me, you get all the resources to build a better life for your pack." Daisy said while standing. She started walking around the table. Xavion blocked her path to me. I signaled him to let her through. He moved aside, and she continued walking towards me. I stood over her and stared down at her. She was beautiful. She was 5'6, with honey skin. She had long straight brown hair and an okay body. I looked into her dark brown eyes and wondered.

"What makes you so confident that I'll make you my wife." I asked.

She smiled. She thought that she was getting to me. "Like I said before, my family has resources that your pack needs. I also come from a strong background of Guardians. We are Mastery Elementals. Meaning I will give you strong sons and daughters. I can be obedient and do whatever is needed. I am one of a kind, Alpha." She finished. I placed my finger under her chin and tilted her head up.

"I don't need an obedient mate. I need a woman that has her own mind and can lead if I am unable to. You. I will have to train. And I don't have the time to do that." I let out a breath and dropped my hand from her chin. "You are not one of a kind. And hear me when I say, that you will never be my wife." I told her and walked around her. "I am already a mated man, Mr. Patterson. I will advise you and your family to forget what you were told." I told them.

"I know you are not talking about that girl. She is not your mate. That was what your parents told you when you were younger. That girl is nothing but bad luck. They are coming for her. They all are. We are trying to save you and the rest of these animals from what Nesida's family couldn't. Your father-" Mr. Vandis stood and spoke with anger. I was in his face before he could let out another word that was going to get him fucked up.

"My father. This is his house. You will respect his home and the animals that reside in it." I growled out with my white eyes glowing. I wrapped my hand around his throat slowly and lifted him into the air. "Now, who is coming for my Queen." I asked while my claws started growing into his skin. Mrs. Vandis jumped up and was about to intervene, but my mother let out her own growl that sat her back down in her seat.

"You do understand that you are setting your people up for failure." Mr. Patterson stood with his eyes turning blue. The wind picked up and the picture of my father dropped off the wall. Xavion and Xander pulled my mother behind them. I dropped Mr. Vandis and faced Mr. Patterson. My claws grew, and my eyes got darker. The picture of my father was lifted and now placed back on the wall. "If I was you, I wouldn't do that again." I said. He stepped back in shock. Matter fact, they all were looking at me in shock.

"What are you?" Mr. Patterson asked with fear.

"He is my Alpha." My Queen said, appearing out of nowhere. I looked over at Xavion and he had a smile on his face. I knew it was him that called her. Everyone looked towards Queen. She was dressed in hospital scrubs. Them damn scrubs were looking good on her. She smiled knowing what I was thinking. I walked over to her and wrapped my arms around her waist.

"Queen," I said before kissing her on the lips. She pulled back with a mischievous smile.

"Alpha, I heard that I was needed." She said.

"Mr. and Mrs. Vandis came over with Mr. and Mrs. Patterson. They said that their daughter Daisy was my wife." I told her.

"Oh, really." She said in surprise. "Well I guess I am.... what."

"You are bad luck, Queen." Xander answered. "You will get these animals killed." He said pointing at his self and Xavion.

Queen looked up at me for confirmation. I hunched my shoulders in response. She faced our guests with a smile. She looked over at Daisy and shook her head. Ma came and grabbed Queen's hand. "This is my daughter-in-law, the Queen of the pack, Patience."

"But, you all will call me Queen." She said in that sexy ass voice. We all were smiling proudly. "Now I believe a question was asked and still there was no answer. Do you need help answering the question?" She said towards Mr. Vandis.

"You stay away from my husband. You and your family have caused nothing but trouble. Ever since you were born, you have been messing up the balance between the two species. You should stay with your own kind." Mrs. Vandis stood and said.

"Her own kind is Xavier." Xander spoke.

I guess Daisy got tired of getting looked over, because she stood and began to talk. "You are not his kind. You are an experiment between two people who didn't know what they wanted. Your mother was a great Guardian, but she failed when she mingled with that wolf. If she would have agreed to the other offers, we wouldn't be here trying to save what is left of this, this," she tried to continue, but the look on my Queen's face forbid it. Red eyes, with black streaks in her honey blonde hair, Queen was showing so much control.

"Hypocrite. That's what you and your family are. You sit here and talk about what my mother has done, but your family is doing all the experimenting. My mother loved my father. You can see it in the way she talked to him. The way she touched him. The way she looked at him. It was with love. I was made from love." Both Chaos and Patience spoke. She walked over to Daisy and stood before her. "You would never be enough for my Alpha and our pack. Stay in your lane little flower." She told her and turned to face Mr. Vandis.

"Where were we?" She tapped her finger on her chin as if she was thinking. "Ahh yes, you were going to tell us what we needed to know." She said to Mr. Vandis. He shook his head and didn't realize that telling Chaos no was something that you didn't do. She was in front of him in seconds and placed her hand on his head. She stared into his eyes and took whatever she wanted. Mrs. Vandis sat there with her mouth open. They all did.

No one knew how strong Queen was. She gave them a glimpse of what she was and that fucked them up. Mr. and Mrs. Patterson didn't say shit after she shut Daisy up. We all stood back and watched my baby work. She just didn't know that I was going to mark her ass tonight. She pulled back with fury in her eyes. "You were the one that went to the Guardian facility. You called me an abomination. You set everything in motion." She growled out with her teeth growing.

"Queen," I called out. I knew what she wanted to do. I felt it. But this was my mother's parents. If she was going to kill them, it wouldn't be in front of her. Queen looked over at me and understood what I was saying. She retracted her teeth and stared at him.

"Bad luck." She said and walked off out of the front door.

"Take care of this," I told my brothers and went after my Queen. I went out of the door and she was gone. *"Where are you, baby?"* I asked.

"I went to the tree, Alpha. I need to be alone." She responded.

"Ok, Queen. Whatever you need. You know that I am here for you." I told her.

"I know." She said.

I turned and saw the Patterson's pulling off. Mrs. Vandis was walking down the steps with her husband. Mr. Vandis fell off the last step and broke his leg. The shit looked like a freak accident. His bone was out of his leg. He was screaming in pain.

"Please help me." Mrs. Vandis yelled.

My brothers both shook their head and stepped over them. "I ain't fucking with that, bruh. Queen said bad luck and that's what his ass got. I don't know if it's contagious or not. To be on the safe side, I ain't touching him." Xavion said jumping in his car. Xander nodded his head in agreement. "No, Ma. Don't touch him. Go inside and call the paramedics." I looked over at them and went to my truck. I wasn't fucking with it either.

~

I knew she told me that she wanted to be alone. I just couldn't help leaving her feeling like that. I stood next to the tree and waited for her to come out. Queen was dealing with a lot of shit. I was happy that she had a handle on Chaos, but no one said anything about the one I saw at the dinner. She looked like a Goddess that should have been standing next to Zeus and shit. I wanted to ask her about it but didn't want to put more pressure on her.

"Vampire." Errol said telepathically.

I started snatching off my clothes and ran into the woods, towards the station. Errol was running things while we were taking care of other stuff. *"How many?"* I growled out. I tuned Dom and the rest of our brothers in.

"Just one. She is with a Guardian. They said that they have information about our Queen. What do you want us to do?" Errol said. I tuned in the rest of the guys in the conversation, while Errol was talking.

"Don't do nothing. Just watch over them until we arrive." I replied.

"What the fuck is going on?" Nick said.

"I don't know? How far are you from the station?" I asked.

"Two minutes." Nick answered.

"I am coming up to the station right now." Xander said.

"I am on the west wing, Xander." Josh said.

"Maxi, go to the tree where we found Queen. Call out to Nico." I told Maxi.

"Ok, Xavion is pulling up from the east side of the station." He responded.

I pulled up in the front of the station with Nick by my side. Our growling parted the circle that was created around the Guardian and the vampire. When we saw who it was, Nick snarled louder and stepped towards the vampire. I shifted back and stood before them with the power of my Elders. "What the fuck are you doing here?" I growled.

"I didn't come here to be mauled by you animals. I am here to see the Queen." She asked. She was unfazed by Nick's growl and my menacing stare. Nick shifted back but still had his claws out.

"What the fuck do you want with my sister?" He asked. We heard more growls around the circle. It opened up and our brothers walked through. The Guardian must have felt the hate pouring out our pores for this vampire. He stepped in front of her and took over.

"She is right. We didn't come here for a fight. We have information about an attack on the Queen." He said.

139

I didn't know who he was, but the vampire behind him, we all knew too well. Kane and Tywain were called to their clan to help take out their clan leader, who fed off of wolves and Guardians. After our grandfather's and some of the Supreme Guardians killed their leader, the vampires blamed the wolves for his blood thrust.

Matteo appeared out of nowhere with black eyes and claws of his own. The vampire hissed at him. The Guardian's eyes changed from dark brown to a green color and he went into attack mode. Matteo smirked at them. "Now you both know that it will take more than the elements and your pointy ass teeth to take me down."

"We are not here to fight." The Guardian said, straightening up. "We have news that the Supremes, council members, and the Guardians assassins are coming your way to kill the Queen. We are here to help." He continued.

"And what is your purpose, Vampire." Matteo spat out. I guess he didn't like them either.

"The same." She replied. She was ready to attack either way.

"Why?" I asked.

She ignored me and kept her eyes on Matteo. "Look, if you let us explain the why, I will. But you will not be going through my head." She told him.

"That's where you fucked up at. You see, I don't need your fucking permission. If you say that your reason for being here is for my granddaughter, you better start talking quick or I will plant little critters into the both of you.

The Guardian stepped forward. He looked like one of the modern ones. He was dressed in the latest fashion, with a mohawk. He had dark skin and was three inches shorter than me. He was sporting two earrings in his ear and tattoos all over his body.

"Don't judge me, man." He told me. "My name is Tyree Normstand. My father is Tarrine Normstand, the Guardian and Supreme of the West. He told me about the prophecy and what it would do for the people. He said that Queen would give each species the balance that has been tampered with from a dark Guardian. This whole time we thought that it was Lord Admerre, better known as Matteo, Dark Matt, but the Supremes and the council members told everyone that you were dead. My father asked over and over, if we could take Queen's energy and use it for our personal gain. The Supremes and the council members disagreed with him. He became enrages and started talking about the Dark Lord will live again. He talked about the Queen and how she will be his.

When the Supremes and the council members saw the damage that was done at the facility, they held another meeting at the west facility. My father didn't want to take her energy this time. He wanted to hold her as a prisoner for some reason. He looked like he has been messing with dark magic. I went to his room to checked on him and overheard him speaking to someone. He told the stranger that his time was almost near and that the Queen will give him what he needed to live again.

I was always against the Guardian's ways. If we didn't live the way they wanted us, we were outlaws and were banned from our families. I pretended to go along with everything that they were saying to get the information that we needed to protect the Queen." He finished.

Matteo turned towards the vampire and frowned. "What impact does she have on your people?"

"If someone with the wrong agenda gets her energy, we all will suffer. Trust me, I am here to help." The vampire stressed.

"In whose hands." Nick asked. She looked over at him with disgust.

"What else is coming that brought you here at this moment?" I asked instead. The Guardian looked around at all the wolves that were surrounding him and the vampire. "Is there a place where we can discuss this?" He asked.

"We can go to the meeting room." Xavion suggested.

I walked into the station with everyone following me. I pulled Errol to the side and gave him orders. "Put a guard around each perimeter of our territory. Place a few guards around my mom's home and make sure to communicate this with Maxi. He has the Queen. Tell him to bring her here when she is finished." I told him. I looked over to Nick and he was giving his pack members orders as well.

I walked into the room after Nick and closed the door. I sat at the head of the table waiting for either the Guardian or the vampire to speak.

The vampire leaned forward and stared across the table at Matteo. "Ma'vere." She whispered.

"What the fuck does Ma'vere have to do with this." Matteo asked.

"I heard my father talking about him to the stranger. He told him that he was going to release him as well." Tyree spoked.

The door opened, and all eyes went to it. Queen walked in with Maxi and Nico behind her. Tyree and the Vampire stood to their feet. "Queen," Tyree spoke.

"I'm sorry, who are you?" She asked. Maxi saw the Guardian and the vampire. He pulled Queen behind him and growled at them both. Nico stood on the side of him with his claws out.

"What the fuck?" Maxi said through clenched teeth.

I got up and went to Queen. "They have information on an attack that will be coming our way. We are trying to find out how the vampires are connected." I told them. I reached out to Queen and she came to me. I wrapped my arms around her waist and brought her closer. "You good." I asked.

"Yeah, I'm good. What attack?" She asked. I grabbed her hand and walked her to the head of the table. I pulled the chair out for her to sit. I stood behind her and waited for the conversation to continue.

Maxi continued growling at the both of them. His eyes were gold and his claws were out. "Calm down, Maxwell." Nick demanded. Maxi was still growling. I looked over to him and it looked like he was trying to calm down. But something was pushing him to the Guardian and the vampire.

"I know you lying." Queen said in shock.

"What, Queen?" I asked.

Maxwell walked to the table and slammed his fist on it. "This can't be fucking happening, bruh." He said through a growl.

I looked over at the vampire and she was fighting the same pull. "Oh, shit." I whispered.

"Nah, that's not fucking happening. Not ever." Josh said. Maxi straightened up and walked to us. "Shock me." He told her.

"Why? She is your mate, Maxi." Queen asked.

'I don't give a fuck. I will not be mating with that." He said angrily.

"What is the big deal?" She asked confusingly.

"SHOCK ME!" He yelled at her.

Tyree and the vampire stood up, ready to attack Maxwell. Queen placed her hand on his arm and shocked the shit out of him.

Maxwell dropped to the ground, shaking. Queen turned to the group pissed. "What the fuck is going on?" She yelled.

"Queen, if I may." Tyree spoked. "We heard that the Guardians are coming for you. We came to help.

"I heard that part already. What the fuck is she?" She asked.

The vampire bowed her head before speaking to her. "Queen, my name is Nylah Loreaux. I am a vampire. Tyree came to our covenant asking about my grandfather Ma'vere. Ma'vere suffered from blood thrust and fed only on Guardians and wolves. He was killed by your grandfather and grandmother."

"Wait. The fuck you talking about. My grandmother didn't have anything to do with this." Maxwell recovered.

"She is not talking about Tywain's wife." Matteo interrupted. "She is talking about mine."

Queen gasped in surprise. This shit was getting crazier by the minute. "Yes, the Guardian of the Light. After they killed him, my family didn't want no one to know that we asked for help. Especially from the weaker ones."

"Who the fuck is you calling weak? Our grandfather took yours out with ease." Xavion spoke.

Nylah shook her head and continued like Xavion didn't speak. "We told the board that the Guardians and the Elder wolves attacked him because of the lives that he had taken. Nothing was done to any of the ones that were involved."

"But that didn't stop the lies and the accusations from the vampires. They called us cowards and told a lot of people that the wolves in the Southern Territory couldn't be trusted." Xander yelled.

"That's enough!" I growled. "We can't change the past. Right now, we got to figure out when they are trying to attack, so that we can get prepared for it."

"Is there anything else that you can tell us about your grandfather that can help us, now." Queen asked. Nylah looked over at Queen with so much respect. She maintained eye contact and talked in a soft tone. "Before my grandfather died, he was in search of the Devil's magic. He was working with one of the Dark Lords in the north. The plan was to kill off all of the Supremes and the Guardian of the Light. Then they were going to take out the wolves. The Dark Lord used old magic. Magic that was generating through his family for years." She told Queen.

Queen looked around at everyone for answers. This was my first time hearing this shit, so I didn't have a clue. Dom shook his head, along with my brothers. Matteo sat with an expressionless face.

"I will find out who she is talking about, but we have to prepare for the Guardians that are coming." Matteo said. "When are they coming exactly?"

"Two weeks." Tyree answered.

"Ok, that is enough time for us to come up with a suitable plan." I said out loud. I turned towards Nylah and Tyree. "If any of you are lying about anything, your deaths will be slow and painful." I sneered.

Maxwell growled at me. Nick looked over at him and frowned. "Trust me, if I can control it, I would. Sorry X." He told me.

"Let's get to work." I said.

TWENTY

Matteo

I couldn't believe what I was hearing. If they were talking about Ma'vere, then the only Guardian that fucked with him like that was the Supreme of Darkness, my teacher, Lord Odom. He taught me about dark magic in France. It was some type of dark magic that was made up from his family. Like my Angel, he didn't have to chant with his magic. I heard that he died along with his clan years before I went in the box. Odom came from a long line of evil muthafuckers. He killed his parents and took over their clan up north. He also had control over some of the rogue wolves. They guarded his gated home and his territory.

I listened to everything that they were saying and none of that shit was going to work. I had to pull Dom and Xavier aside and come up with something ourselves. Because I didn't know if I could trust the Guardian or the vampire yet.

Especially the vampire.

I motioned for Xavier and Dom to step outside. Xavier bent down and whispered something in Angel's ear. She nodded her head and turned back to the conversation at the table. He was trying his hardest to stay on her good side. Everything he did, she knew about.

"Angel got that fool head gone." I said to myself. They followed me out of the door. Xavier continued walking to his office. We followed him in for more privacy. When we got there, Dom started talking.

"I don't trust them two. Is there any way that we can find out if their story is legit or not?"

"I'm already on it. I need to know more about the Dark Lord that Tarrine has been talking to. It will take a whole lot of energy to revive anyone from the dead and the only one with that energy is Queen. We got to figure out if they are coming to kill or capture her." I said.

"It doesn't matter. They won't be doing neither." Xavier growled.

"Yes, it does. It tells us who we are up against and which way our plan should go." I told him.

"So, where do we start." Nick asked.

"We have to create a battlefield and put them all in one spot so that it will be easier to take them out." I told them.

"The only field we have that is big enough for that type of battle is next to this station." Xavier answered.

"Ok, well it starts here." I told them. Xavier gave us an outline of his whole territory. The open spot was going to give us the advantage but we all had to figure out how we were going to protect all the wolves. Guardians were able to freeze and kill them on the spot. Angel and I could control their freeze along with Tyree. But like I said before, I didn't trust him yet.

"If you guys can hold off their freeze and their magic against us, we can take them all out quickly." Dom said.

"What if some of them don't come to the field? What if they go to your home looking for her?" Xavier asked.

"If they are tracking her here, they will track her magic. She could leave traces of her magic in the field and they should come running. I just want all of the Supremes present, including the council members. They won't show until they have proof of her being captured or her death." I told them. Xavier growled at that statement.

Tyree walked in on our conversation. "My father has called for another meeting before the attack. I was going to attend it to make sure that none of their plans will change." He said.

"Good, I will come with you." I stood and told him. "This way, I wouldn't have to go through your head and dig out the information myself. "

"I told you that I was here for the Queen. I will never go against her." Tyree told me. I could see it in his eyes that he was telling the truth. I wondered if he was here for my granddaughter in other ways. I looked over at Xavier and he was mean mugging Tyree. Dom was too. But Xavier's eyes were flicking white and black.

"Calm down, man. Are you that insecure about yo shit, that you don't trust her." Tyree spoked.

I didn't see when Xavier took the steps to get in his face. "I trust her. I don't trust you."

"If you trust her, then you have nothing to worry about." Tyree sighed. "We don't have time for you to figure yo shit out within yourself. Shit will get messed up real quick if we don't come up with a plan. If you saw what I saw, then you would understand where I am coming from." Tyree spoke with dread in his voice.

"How did you see this? The vampire showed you." I asked him. He let out a deep breath before nodded his head.

"Do you think that she manipulated the vision somehow, to make you see what she wanted you to see." Dom spoked.

"I don't think so. There were things that she knew about my father before I told her anything. She knew that he was talking to a Dark Lord, but the Dark Lord had blinded his self from her visions. We didn't have time to investigate it." He told her.

"Follow me." I told them. I went back into the meeting room where everybody was gathered. Maxi was still getting shocked by Angel to interrupt the mating call. I didn't blame him. I wouldn't want to be tied down to a disloyal ass family either. I walked over to Angel and stood next to her. "Show Angel what you saw." I told the vampire.

"Fuck no! My sister is not going into her mind. We don't want her to tell her stupid ass people that we forced her to do shit." Maxi snarled.

"Right now, we don't have a choice. They trust Angel. If they want to gain our trust, she will have to go in her mind and find the truth." I told Maxwell. He was shaking his head along with Xavier. "I don't trust this shit either."

"Let her see it through me then." Tyree suggested. Without hesitation or approval from anyone, he walked over to her and kneeled. He put his head down and waited for her to go through his mind. Angel looked over at Xavier for permission. He thought on it for a minute before he nodded his head. Angel placed her hand on Tyree's head. I placed my hand on her shoulder and we went through his thoughts together. She went through each door in his head and I followed. She came up to a memory of a vision and waited for it to be seen. The vision cleared and there was a shadow figure, wearing a black cloak, walking around in a house. I heard Angel gasp and saw the picture of her father and Nesida on the floor. This was her family's home. The shadow was tall and powerful. Written spells and black magic circled around it. He stood over something that was eating something. We both moved around it and saw a blood thrust Ma'vere eating on a wolf. I looked around and saw the bodies of Angel's family on the ground drained of their blood. When he picked his head up, his eyes were red, and magic was seen running through his veins.

The shadow turned around and walked to the window of the house. When he looked out of it, the land that used to be green with flowers and trees, were now ashes and ruins. Bodies were spread out all over the Southern Territory.

"We did it my Queen." The shadow said. Angel and I looked over in the direction that he was speaking and saw my Angel's body shriveled up and drained of her blood.

Angel broke the connection. She stood and walked off into the corner. Xavier walked over to her and wrapped his arms around her. I turned to the vampire with a glare on my face. "How accurate are your visions?"

"The visions are accurate as long as everything goes as planned. If something happens between time, the vision will change." Nylah replied.

"How long ago was this vision?" I asked.

"This vision happened a year ago. I didn't think nothing of it, because we thought that the Queen had died. But, when we heard that she was alive and was about to mate with the Alpha of the Southern Territory, I knew it was her." She said, staring over in the corner where my Angel was. She was standing next to a shocked Xavier with her golden hair and white eyes. She looked over the room with a fearless calm and said, "That won't be happened. I guarantee it." She said with a knowing smile.

Patience

After we confirmed what Tyree and Nylah had been telling us, we had been strategizing plans every night. I knew that I would give my life for my family to live. I also knew that it was going to be hard for them to get over my death, but I needed to make sure that they were safe. I told my Papi not to tell anyone what we saw. I wanted to keep it between us. Xavier asked me repeatedly about what had happened in Tyree's mind. I didn't want him to worry and lose focus on the pack or his brothers. I knew he would have picked me over everyone, but I didn't want to put him in that position.

We have been going through ideas for three days. Tyree came back and told us that they were still coming but the council members were staying behind, just like Papi said. We now had to get them all in one spot. After the fourth night, we still didn't get nowhere. I came home with Nico and Nylah. She didn't want to leave my side and I was fine with that. She was fucking with Maxi's senses. He kept asking me to shock him. The last time I did it, Nylah hissed at me. She apologized and shook her head.

Xavier, Dom, and Papi were still going over their plan with the rest of the pack and Tyree. I told them that I wanted to check on things at the hospital with Camryn and Treasure. I found out yesterday, that she was going to give birth any day now. Our full term of pregnancy was at four months. Shifter babies grew quicker than the average babies. Josh was so excited. Shit we all were. Nylah and I shadowed Cam all day. Anything that she needed, we got for her. "You guys, let me breathe." She told us.

"Not a chance. You are lucky that Josh let you come to work." I told her.

"Yeah, but let's see how y'all are going to act when Treasure gives birth to the next Alpha." Cam said with a smirk. I looked over at Treasure and she was giving Cam the evil eye. "She was going to find out soon anyway." Cam said.

"Treasure," I whispered. She glanced over at me and smile.

"What sis?" I walked over to her with my hand out.

"Can I?" I asked. She let out a sigh and turned her body towards me. I placed my hand on her stomach and felt three heartbeats. One of them being Treasures and the other two were their boys. I placed my hand on my chest with surprise and felt something odd. I dropped my hand to my stomach and felt another rapid heartbeat.

"Oh shit." I whispered.

"What's wrong Patience?" Treasure said with fear.

"Nothing, they are healthy. Your baby boys are strong and healthy." I said.

"Oh my God." Treasure replied. "Two of them."

"Yep, two stubborn bad ass lil wolves." I told her.

"So, you know what that means for you, huh? Bed rest." Cam said and started laughing. I smiled but was still shocked at what I found out. Nylah was looking at me funny. She walked over and stood in front of me.

"Is everything alright Queen?" She asked.

"Yeah, I guess I am a little tired. I didn't get enough sleep last night." I replied and walked off to the bathroom. I didn't want to discuss this with no one yet. I knew that they were going to need my help in the battle. If I told Xavier about the baby, he would have banned me from the battlefield and that was something that I couldn't let happen.

After Treasure and Camryn's shift was over, we went over to Dom's house. Jess met us over there with Loreen and Tori. Camryn and Treasure started dinner, while my crazy ass friends asked Nylah questions.

"So, if you bite me, will I change into a vampire." Tori asked.

Nylah answered her with no emotion. "No."

"So, if you bite me, you just going to suck all on my neck and drain me dry." Tori asked, with a stank face.

"No." Nylah replied.

"What you mean no? Girl you don't know what you are missing. I eat good. My blood tastes sweet and delicious." Tori said.

"How are you going to get mad because that girl doesn't want to bite you? You know if she shows you her teeth, your ass gon' start screaming. Sit yo ass down somewhere." I told her. She was always extra with meeting new people. What bothered me the most, was the silence of Loreen. She was extra quiet about Nylah being a vampire. I knew my homegirl would have grilled Nylah just like Tori was. "What's wrong with you?" I asked her.

She looked over at me and sighed. "Nothing, P. I just got a lot on my mind." She answered. I looked over at Tori and Jess. They came and sat closer to us. We always knew when there was something wrong. Jess put her arm around Loreen and asked her again. "What's wrong Sis? You know that we can't help if you don't tell us what is wrong."

"Y'all know that I was kind of skeptical about fucking around with Xavion. But, we started something up after the trip in New Orleans. We slept in the same room without doing anything. We just talked all night about my childhood and how he grew up. The other night he invited me over to his house and y'all know that I was down for some Netflix and chill. I put on one of those sundresses with nothing underneath. When I pulled up, he was waiting at the door for me. I couldn't get to the door all the way, y'all. Xavion snatched my ass out of the doorway and placed me on the open door. He stuck his tongue in my mouth and I was grinding on his thick piece. He kicked the door shut and carried me to the bedroom.

Xavion rubbed and caressed my body for ten minutes. I was wet and begging for it at that point. He told me that he was going to taste me later because he needed to be inside me. As soon as he pushed inside of me, he called out another girl's name. I tried to push him off of me, but his ass started getting wild. I reached for the lamp that was by the bed and smashed it on the side of his head. He got up and started growling and shit. I ran out the bedroom and out that fucking house. He been calling me since then, but I am not answering for him. He could keep his punk ass away from me." She told us.

I knew she was hurting about it and playing it off like she didn't care. My sister was hurting bad too. I couldn't wait to see Xavion. I was going to fuck his ass up.

"Don't worry about it, sis. We are going to get him for you. Just sit back and enjoy the show." Tori told her. She nodded her head, but you could see that she didn't want us to do anything to Xavion. I was going to talk to Xavier about this shit. Dom walked in with Josh and Maxi. Maxi looked over at Nylah and growled. "Why is she in our home?"

"I will be wherever the Queen will be. Get used to it." She hissed out. Maxi got in front of her and looked down at her.

"Watch your fucking mouth when you are talking to me." Nylah looked up at him and her red eyes were glowing with her fangs showing. "And who are you exactly." She asked. We all stared at them and waited for Maxi to respond. We knew that he wasn't going to hit her. Well at least we hoped he didn't. His chest was going in and out. Nylah licked her lips and Maxi moaned. He stepped closer to her and leaned in to whisper in her ear.

"I'll be the one that make you scream in pleasure and pain. Fuck with it if you want." He told her and nipped her ear with his wolf teeth. Nylah's eyes closed, and she inhaled his scent. She wanted Maxi in the worst way. Maxi smirked at her in a taunting way and walked off. Nylah was trying to recover.

"So, are you going to fuck with it or what?" I asked.

The girls started laughing and Nylah couldn't do nothing but shake her head. Whether she liked it or not, she was now family. I hoped she had hair all over to feed into Maxi's fetish. I went to the kitchen to help Treasure and Cam. I didn't think Dom knew about the twins. He was holding her from behind, while Cam was sitting in Josh's lap. I went over to the kitchen island where all the food was sitting on. I gathered the plates and started piling food onto them. Jessica and Tori came in to help. Xavier and the rest of the guys were on their way. We usually went to Nanny's house to eat, but Elder Locklear was there to counsel Ms. Robin and Nico. Nico told her that he wasn't for all that waiting. He was ready to be with her and she needed to get ready.

I placed Dom's and Treasure's plate in front of them. Treasure's plate had more on it. Dom smiled up at me. "You know, huh?"

"Yeah, I know. Them boys are going to give you the same hell that you used to give Momma and Daddy." I told him.

Dom sat back and looked up at me. He grabbed Treasure's face and stared up into her eyes. She smiled sweetly at him. He tugged on her bottom lip while maintaining eye contact.

"No more work. From now on, you are staying home." He told her and pushed her plate to the side. He scooped up a spoonful of mashed potatoes from his plate and placed it in her mouth. "Good girl." He whispered.

"I told you." Cam said while Josh fed her.

"You talking all that shit, but today was your last day. You won't be going back to work for a while. Because after this one, you are going to be pregnant again." Josh told her. Treasure poked her tongue at Cam and started laughing. I was happy that no one knew about my baby. I knew that I would have been laying in the bed with Treasure and Cam's asses. Loreen came stomping in the kitchen with a frown on her face. She walked over to us and squeezed her ass in between me and Jess. We already knew what was up. I put the plate down and picked up a knife. Jess picked up the rolling pin and Tori took her mace out of her purse.

Xavion stormed in with crazed eyes. He looked over at us and glared at Loreen. "Why are you making this so difficult? I just want to talk to you." He growled. I didn't understand why he was so upset with her not wanting to talk to him. It wasn't like she was his mate. "Leave me the fuck alone Xavion. Go talk to that bitch, Eve." Loreen replied. Xavion moved forward and I stepped in front of Loreen. "Back off Xavion." I told him. His wolf eyes were flashing. It looked like he wanted to move, but something was preventing him to do so. Xavion swiped the food off the counter and growled at me.

Dom picked Treasure up and placed her behind him. Josh did the same with Cam. Maxi came from the back door with his claws out. Xavier and Xander came through the door ready to take Xavion down. I didn't need them to do shit. Xavion was like a brother to me. So, whatever had him like this, was fucking with him on a deeper level. Without wasting any time, I stilled him and placed my hand on his head.

"Shhhh," I told him. His eyes were still a little glossy and they were looking through me. I looked in his mind and saw a black cloud covering it. I wanted to lift it, but I would have to consume it into myself before I can release it. I was pregnant and already had a lot going on with myself. I didn't need extra shit to fight off. I pulled at it and Xavion started screaming.

"Let me, Sis." I heard Chaos asked. I took one step back and she put one foot forward. I closed my eyes and concentrated on the cloud in his mind. Chaos pulled at one stitch and the whole cloud came tumbling down. I pulled back with my eyes on Xavion. Black stuff was leaking out of his eyes. Loreen grabbed some paper towels and came over to Xavion. She wiped at his face and he stared at her like he was seeing her for the first time.

"Are you ok?" Loreen asked him.

"Lo, Lo, Lo-Eve." Xavion said. Loreen mushed his face and went off. "Are you serious right now?" She yelled. "Fuck this shit." She turned and walked off. Xavion tried to grab her but she slapped the fuck out of him.

"Loreen stop! It is not what you think. Trust me, if it was something like what we were thinking, I would have fucked him up." I told her.

She looked over at me with tears in her eyes. She was hurting behind whatever was affecting Xavion. You could see that he wanted her and tried to call out her name. I needed to find out who this bitch Eve was.

"AHH," Cam yelled. We all looked over at her.

Josh's goofy ass stood over there, looking scared as fuck. "Hey, bruh. Get yo shit together and let's go." Maxi yelled. That got Josh's attention and moving. He picked Cam up and ran out of the door. We all ran after him, forgetting everything else that was going on. Maxi even gave Nylah a ride in his truck. We got back to the hospital within fifteen minutes. Josh pulled up and jumped out with Cam, with the truck still in drive. Dom jumped in and stopped it from running into another truck.

"Stupid ass." He mumbled.

"Yeah, you are going to be just like that." Xavier told him with a smile. Dom smiled and went into the hospital with the rest of the group. I began to follow when Xavier pulled me back. "I can't get a kiss or nothing from my Queen. I thought I told you about that." He teased. I leaned into him and wrapped my arms around his neck.

"No, you told me to never leave without kissing or hugging you."

"I didn't know that I needed to tell you that." Xavier teased. He looked at me and inhaled my scent. "It's funny how my scent is all over you and we haven't been together for a couple of days." He told me before he stuck his face in my neck.

"I guess you were right. No matter what I do, I will always be yours." I responded calmly. He stared into my eyes looking for the truth behind those words. I didn't lie.

"Aye, you two coming in." Xander yelled out the door.

Xavier reached down and grabbed my hand while staring at me. He pulled me towards the entrance door to the hospital. We got onto the elevator with Xander and Jess. Xavier was still staring at me and I hoped that he didn't figure out that I was pregnant. When we got on the maternity floor, we heard someone yelled and growled. Dom and Maxi were pacing back and forth. Nylah was standing on the side, while everyone else sat and waited. I wasn't going to sit out here and wait for shit. I ran to the door and went in.

Cam was breathing in and out heavily, with Treasure and Josh at her side. I walked over to Cam and touched her leg.

"Breathe," I told her.

She leaned back, and her breathing became calm. I kept my hand on her leg while the doctors worked on getting my nephew out. She pushed out a 9-pound baby, without any pain.

"Baby sis, I want your ass in here when I go into labor. You are better than an epidural." Treasure told me. Josh kissed Cam all over her face.

"You are amazing." Josh told her with awe. I have never seen my brother like this. He was gentle and soft. The same way my father used to be with my mother. The nurse walked over with the baby and placed him on her chest.

"Hey big man." Cam whispered in tears. "I am your Mommy."

The baby started moving but settled back on her chest with a small smile. Josh grabbed his little hand and kissed it. "I'm your Daddy." He said tenderly. The baby opened his golden eyes and stared at his proud Poppa. "That's my boy." Josh said and kissed him on the forehead.

The knocking on the door didn't interrupt their moment. Everyone walked in and looked down on the new addition to the family. "Name your son, baby?" Camryn told Josh with her eyes still on the baby. Josh smiled and responded.

"When we were young, we asked Poppa why he didn't name us after him. He said, he wanted us with our own name. I understood what he was saying but I told him that I will name my first son after a great man." He looked up at Dominick and Maxie. "My son will be named after two great men. Dominick Maxi Black."

Dom and Maxi walked over to their nephew and brother. They gave each other that brotherly hug and dapped each other off. I took a step back and watched the interaction with my family. My brothers were smiling, laughing, and celebrating life. I came in and fucked that up. I had put them all in danger by bringing this foolishness to their doorstep. I felt him before he could come closer. "After this is over, that will be you. You know that right." He asked while wrapping his arms around me from behind.

"I would like to be mated and married first, Alpha." I tilted my head and looked into his eyes. "I love you, Alpha. I love you so much." I told him. His face frowned up with confusion.

"Queen."

"Hey sis, come over here and meet your nephew." Josh yelled out to me. I tried to walk out of Xavier's arms, but he tightened his grip. I looked up at him with pleading eyes. He walked over with me and watched as I held my beautiful nephew. You couldn't tell who he looked like right now, but he did have our cognac eyes, which were now staring up at me. "Hi, my little nephew. I am your Guardian, T Patience." I whispered, and he smiled. "I will protect you, little one."

TWENTY-ONE

Xavier

J knew that she was holding something back from me. I wanted to hear her say it and not have to go through her mind. Matteo and Queen had been whispering shit to each other and that shit was pissing me off. I told her ass no more secrets and her ass didn't listen. We were in the same bed again last night talking about our future. She asked me how many kids I wanted and when I wanted to start. She just didn't know that I was trying to get her pregnant asap and keep her that way.

The next day, we talked about how we planned on setting the Guardians and the council members up. The plan sounded solid. It was two days before the attack and we were all just chilling with the family. Mom cooked a big dinner and we were all sitting around eating and talking. Nylah was standing in the corner watching over Queen and Maxi. She wasn't slick.

"Let me hold my grandson, please." Ma told Camryn. She had been at the house with Cam and Josh every night. When the baby started crying, Ma got up, fed him, and rocked him back to sleep. She said that she was going to do that for the first month. After that, they were on their own.

She took Dominick from Josh's arms and started rocking him. It didn't make any sense, because the baby was already sleeping. "Ma, you are spoiling him. Why don't you lay him down?" I told her.

"Because there is no rule for Grandmothers. We can spoil our babies rotten and you can't tell me nothing. You need to worry about making me more grandbabies to spoil." She told me with her eyes still on the baby.

"Trust me, it will be sooner than later." I said while gripping Queen's leg under the table. She glanced over at me and smiled.

"Oh, are you serious." Jess said.

"Serious about what." Queen replied.

"Girl you are pregnant and didn't tell us!" Tori yelled.

I looked at Queen with a frown on my face. She was really going to get fucked up if she was and didn't tell me first. "Are you Queen?" I grilled.

"No, I am not pregnant. Come on guys, really." She replied but didn't make eye contact with me. I didn't understand why she would lie to me about something as important as this. Jess, understanding that this was something that Queen didn't want to talk about, changed the subject.

"Ma, when are you and Nico's mating ceremony. I want to be far away after the ceremony." Everyone started laughing but me and Queen's brothers. They know that something was off as well but couldn't put their finger on it. I moved my hand off her leg and placed it on her stomach. She looked over at me and stared. The only heartbeat that I felt was hers, but her scent was different. Queen placed her hand on mine and removed it. She continued listening to Ms. Robin and Jessica's conversation.

"Our mating ceremony will be in Florida, two weeks from now. We want a different scenery and thought that after everything that had happened, we will all need a vacation." Ms. Robin spoke.

"You are not lying. I haven't been out of Louisiana since I made it my home. We all are going. You too, Nylah and Tyree. You are family now." Ma said.

"She not going nowhere with us Nanny. After all this is over, she can carry her ass right back to her covenant." Maxi replied before Nylah could say anything.

"Be careful, Maxwell. You keep talking for me, people are going to think that you care." Nylah told him.

"Trust me, I don't. Besides, I don't think my date would mind." He said before picking up his drink.

Nylah smiled. "That's great. I wouldn't want Queen to have to shock you when you see my date feeding off me. Things can get exciting when I am bitten." Nylah told him with lust in her eyes.

Maxi's glass broke in his hand. He stood with a growl and walked over to Nylah. Maxwell grabbed her and dragged her out the back door. We all started laughing. It was going to be trouble getting them two together. "Hey, we gotta make sure that we have everything set up for the battle. We don't want anything to go wrong. Treasure and Cam, what time are y'all pulling out tomorrow." Nick asked them.

"We are planning on leaving at three. The hospital is already cleared out. All the travel doctors and nurses will be on call in Slidell. When the battle is over, we will wait for the ok to come back. Dr. Turner and Dr. Buras with a couple of RNs will be closer by for all of the wounded." Treasure answered.

"Jess, where are you guys going." Queen asked.

"We are going to Slidell as well. Xander and Nico don't want us close by." Jess answered.

We continued with dinner without Maxi and Nylah. Tyree was glancing over at Tori, but she looked uninterested. Xavion was under Loreen all night. Queen told us about the black cloud that was in his head. She looked in his head earlier and didn't see it there anymore, but it was over his heart. Queen didn't want to tamper with that until she was sure that it wouldn't hurt him. Loreen stood by his side the whole time. "When I catch that bitch, I am going to fuck her up." Queen growled.

"Well, I am going into the city. Mardi Gras is the best time that I can be myself." Matteo jumped up, interrupting my thoughts. "Anyone wants to come along."

"Sure, I haven't been on Bourbon Street in years." Tyree said. "Do you want to join us?" He held his hand and asked Tori. She looked over at Jess and Loreen. "Are y'all coming?"

"No, we are going to stay away from Bourbon Street until we can find out who did this to Xavion." Loreen answered. Xavion stood up with her and said their goodbyes.

"Sure, I don't mind if it's okay with my husband." Jess said smiling at Xander.

"Whatever you want sweetheart." He told her with a kiss on the lips.

Jess turn towards us. "Hey, do you two have any plans."

"Yes, we do." Queen answered.

"We do?" I asked in shock.

"You'll see." She said in a singing tone. Jess and the girls around the table started giggling. My brothers all looked confused like me. "Well, this is a discussion that I don't want to be a part of. Let's go kids. Nico and Robin, bring y'all ass on too." Matteo told them and walked out the door. Tori grabbed Tyree's hand and followed Matteo out with the rest of the couples. Ma and Queen got up to clear the table. Cam and Treasure went to help them out. It was just me, Nick, and Josh at the table.

"What's going on with my sister, bruh?" Nick asked me.

"I don't know, man. We have been talking and getting along fine. I feel that she is lying to me about something. I just don't know what yet." I told him.

"Well, she told us that she had a surprise for us and was going to show us after all this bullshit is over. Do you think it is about that?" Josh questioned.

"No, it doesn't have anything to do with that." I responded. Queen walked in smiling at me.

"Are you ready to go?"

"Yes, Queen." I stood and dapped my brothers off. "I'll see you guys tomorrow."

"Not too early." Nick said with a mischievous smile. I shook my head at him and went into the kitchen.

"See you tomorrow Ma." I kissed her on the cheek and gave her a big hug.

"Alright baby." She told me.

I told the rest of the women goodbye and kissed my lil nephew.

Queen was waiting for me outside next to my truck. I walked over and opened the door. She shook her head and started undressing herself.

"Can we go for a run?" She asked. Queen raised her hands up and lifted her head to the sky, with her eyes close. It looked like she was testing the air. The wind picked up and her eyes opened at me. They were lighter than her usual color. She smiled at me and her beautiful honey blonde, shiny fur started sprouting out. She fell on all fours and howled out to the moon. The white streaks made it look like she had diamonds in her fur. Her hazel eyes looked up at me. *"What are you waiting on?"* She asked. I ripped off my clothes and shifted into my wolf. Queen took off running, begging for me to chase her.

I howled out to the moon and to anyone that was in the woods tonight. I received a few howls back, letting me know that we had the woods to ourselves. I sprinted in the direction Queen went. Queen was fast, even when she was playing around. She was always up for a challenge. I got to the lake where we made love for the first time. She didn't understand how much that night meant to me. I smelled her before she came out of the woods on my right. She was a woman again. She walked over with her hips swaying. I became captivated and wanted to taste every drop of her. I shifted back and grabbed her waist. I pulled her body to me and placed soft kisses on her neck. She moaned and pulled my face in deeper. I was about to lay her down, but she stopped me. I looked at her and saw that we were in our bedroom.

"Not this time, Alpha. Let me show you." She said. Her eyes were a mixture of red, white, and hazel color. I took a step back.

"Queen," I asked confusingly.

"It's me Alpha. Like you told me before. I have to accept all that I am." She grabbed my hand and led me to the bed. I sat down with my eyes on hers. "Let us take care of you, Alpha." She moaned out with need. I stretched out on the bed and let them do what they wanted to do. She crawled between my legs with desire in her eyes. She sat up on her knees and placed her hands on my thighs.

"OH SHIIIT!" I groaned out. I felt her lips everywhere. She

was biting on my neck and chest at the same time. I opened my eyes and she was still sitting on her knees smiling at me.

"You were right, sis. He likes this very much." I heard her say.

"What else she told you I like?"

She licked those beautiful lips. "She said you loved the way my mouth work." She leaned forward and wrapped her lips around the tip of my dick. "Mmm, Alpha you taste real good." She said before she placed my entire length down her throat without any breaks.

"Fuuuck, Queen." I yelled out with no shame. The biting was getting harder and the kisses were getting more passionate all over my body. I lifted my head up to watch her. She went up and down without any breaks. I thrust up and she groaned out in response. Queen began to roll her tongue around my dick and I felt myself getting close. She placed her hands on her back and sucked harder. "That's it baby." I told her and exploded in her mouth.

She sat up and stared down at me with her colorful eyes. She bit her bottom lip and touched my leg again. All of the kissing and biting stopped. Queen came forward and placed soft kisses on my stomach and worked her way up. She straddled my body and began to rub her warm wet center across my dick teasingly. I knew that she wanted control tonight, but I didn't like this teasing shit. I grabbed her hips and pulled her down.

"Alpha," she said my name with relief. I pulled her down for a kiss and she began bouncing on my dick. I moved her body to the side so that I can watch her ass go up and down.

"Cum for me Queen." I demanded and slapped her ass.

"I'm right there, King." She yelled. I felt her walls get tighter and wetter.

"Queen," I moaned out as we both reached our orgasm. We both were breathing heavy with our eyes closed. She rolled on the side of me and started giggling. I opened my eyes and gazed into her cognac ones. "What was that all about?" I asked her.

"We all love you Xavier." She replied.

"Who is the we, Queen? I know Chaos, but who is the other one?"

"She is me." Queen responded.

"I don't get it." I said and sat up. This shit was confusing.

She sat up with me to explain. "Chaos is the Guardian of the Dark. Patience is the Guardian of the Light. I learned how to pull my magic from my heart and not from hate. When I found out what you have been doing, I didn't want to harm you and regret it, so my heart reacted. That was why you were still standing at dinner."

"Wow babe. You have complete control over both sides." She nodded her head with an excited smile. All I could do was smile back at her. I was proud of my Queen; she was going to fuck those Guardians up.

~

We all met up in the middle of the field the next day. Queen was leaving traces of her magic in the woods to lead the Guardians there. After sharing that special night with her, something was still off. Tyree and Nylah walked up right before Queen came into view with Nico and Maxi.

"Hey Tyree, where is Matteo. He didn't come back in the bar last night."

"I told you that he met up with some woman." He replied.

"I thought you told us that he was tired and went home." Nico said. We all looked at Tyree. He smirked and teleported to Queen. Nylah moved to Nico and kicked him back into the woods. Tyree grabbed Queen's wrist and placed a bracelet on it.

"What the fuck are you doing?" I growled. I felt my eyes changing and the darkness that I consumed from Chaos was coming through.

"We are taking her to the Western Facility. She won't be able to contain this power. Chaos is getting stronger by the minute and when she does, we will all die. That is not a risk that I am willing to take." Tyree said angrily.

"You punk ass bitch. We trusted you." Nick growled out.

"That was the point." Nylah said. Maxwell shifted into his wolf and leaped at her. Tyree held his hand out and stilled him.

"Stay." Tyree told Maxwell. Josh and Xander wanted to shift, but they knew that he was going to still them as well. I held my hand out for them to wait.

I looked over at Queen for a sign or something. She was sweating, and she was getting pale.

"Oh, she can't use her magic. Not with these on." Tyree told me and pointed to the bracelet.

"I will rip your fucking head off. You and the rest of your family will die." I told him. He looked surprised. My eyes were now black, and my claws were longer.

"You gotta catch me first." He said right before Queen passed out in his arms. I teleported behind him and swiped my hand down. I missed.

She was gone. I felt my blood pumping faster through my veins. I couldn't believe I let this happen. My Queen was gone and there was no way of getting her back. I dropped my head back and screamed out in pain.

"FUUUCK!"

TWENTY-TWO

Patience

"*T*hank you, Tyree. You have earned your spot on the board. Come, sit with us and watch the death of this error." Amere said to Tyree. He was the council member that I saw talking to the Supreme in the Southern Territory. He was there that night when my parents were killed. I remembered seeing him in the shadows. Tyree took his seat and stared at me.

This was some straight up bullshit. I woke up in the middle of the Western Facility with my hands chained down to the floor and a black collar around my neck. I didn't know what to expect around these Guardians. They were all looking at me like I was an exhibit in the Museum.

"She looks just like her mother, but I can see the evilness that is awake in you, child." One of them spoke. I didn't say anything to none of them. I just sat there and let them say whatever.

"Did you have help with destroying the Southern Facility?"

"Have you had any contact with your grandfather?" One of the council members spoke this time. I was in a wide room surrounded by tables and chairs. The council members were seated on the left and the right side of the three main Supremes that sat in the middle. One of them was Tyree's father Tarrine. There were other

Guardians circled around me. I didn't know where Nylah went. I tugged on the chains and they bit into my skins. I tried reaching out to Xavier and my brothers, but they were blocking my magic.

"Since you don't want to answer any of our questions, do you have anything to say before you are judged?" The one that sat in the middle spoke. I heard the other Guardians praying for a slow death so that I can suffer. I focused on the middle Supreme and asked a question.

"Why did you kill my parents?" I asked in a weak voice.

"Your magic is uncontrollable. We tried to tell this to your mother, but she promised us that she was going to keep you under control. When we heard of the incident with that wolf boy and other disturbing things, we knew that our decision wasn't wrong. We should not have trusted Nesida and her wolf. If they would have killed you that night a long time ago, I wouldn't have to bury my brothers." He shouted.

"I do think that we should explore this energy. She is of the unknown. Just think of the power that us Guardians can have." Tarrine leaned over and told the Supreme that sat in the middle.

"I don't want this type of magic in none of my brothers." The Supreme responded. He stood with the rest of the Guardians and the council members. The Supreme in the middle started chanting and the rest of them joined in, except Tarrine. His eyes had dark circles around them and his skin was saggy. I didn't know how others weren't seeing how much he was changing. The dark magic ate at him.

Tarrine raised his hands and black smoke came from them. He shot it towards the two Supremes.

"I am sorry brothers, but I can't let you kill her. She is too valuable to just kill. The Dark Lord awaits her."

"Are you mad Tarrine? You can't trust the Dark Lord. He will suck you dry and leave you lifeless. Don't be a fool." A council member yelled.

"No, his plan is to suck you all dry." Tarrine replied. The Supremes dropped and Tarrine was rejuvenated. He looked younger than his son. He walked forward and faced the council members. "We can rule the world with the Dark Lord. He has forgiven us and wishes to live amongst us."

"Do you know how stupid you sound right now? He cannot be trusted." Someone yelled.

"This isn't up for debate." He said and turned towards me with black eyes. "It will only be painful, if you fight it."

"We will not let this happen." A Guardian came forward and threw a gust of wind at Tarrine. He countered it with his own and sent the Guardian to the wall head first. Everyone heard his neck break on impact. The other Guardians started attacking him. The council members teleported out their seats and were now standing around me. Tyree was standing in my sight. His face was frowned up and looked uncertain about the turn of events.

"Amere, let's finished this the old school way." Another council member said.

Amere walked forward and pulled out an old sword. It was the same one that killed my father. I would never forget that blade. It had Guardian's writings all over it. He unlatched the collar that was around my neck and began to chat. Tarrine was still fighting off the Guardians and some of the assassins joined in. The heaviness of the collar made my head drop forward. Amere began to chat with the rest of the council members and was about to swing the blade. It hit an invisible barrier which caused a spark. Amere looked around to see what interrupted the blade from connecting with my neck.

A deep, dark laugh was heard around the room. Everyone stopped and looked around. The Guardians and the assassins that were fighting Tarrine backed up and looked around as well. "Do you really think that I was going to let you weak fucks kill my grand-child." Papi said in an unnerving voice. The council members looked back at me. I smiled and released myself from the chains.

"That is impossible. Your magic should have been blocked." Amere said in fear.

"You are pathetic. You thought that these weak chains can hold down a Queen." I taunted.

Papi appeared next to me in his Dark Lord form. His eyes were all black and his skin was ashen. He still looked his age but scarier.

"I told you that they were stupid. They thought that they could hold me and my magic in a box." He said in a deep voice. All eyes were on us. Tyree stepped forward and stood by my side.

"Queen," he said.

"Good job, Tyree. Now let's finish this off." I told him. Papi didn't waste no time. He started throwing black masses with electric currents around them, at all the council members except for Amere. He was going to be mine. The assassins came towards me. Tyree jumped in front of me and started fighting them off with his magic and something that looked like a lightning bolt. Nylah appeared and snatched the head off an assassin that was behind Tyree. They began going around the room shedding the blood of every Guardian there.

Little dark shadow figures were coming from the ground and formed into critters. They started attacking the other Guardians that was coming towards us from other angles. Papi was going around snapping necks and tearing limbs off bodies. He had it on his mind for a long time. I told him if I was able to kill the Guardian that was at the table with the Supremes, he could have everyone else.

I glanced over at Amere. He held the blade in his left hand, as his right hand held an electric ball. I wasn't in the mood to drag his death out. I wanted all of this to be over, so that I can go to my King.

"You will not survive this child." He told me and swung the blade at me. I moved to the right, where he was aiming the electric ball. "Goodbye." He said and let the ball loose.

The ball stopped in front of me, waiting for instructions. His mouth dropped open. "You underestimated me, I see Amere." I said in my chiming voice. "You knew my mother well. You knew that you or anyone else wouldn't be able to kill her, so you told them to kill my father. You knew what it would have done to her, but you didn't know what it would have done to me. You saw a power that surpassed yours and the rest of the members of the council board. That's why you ran back to the council members and the rest of the

Supremes. You got scared of a six-year-old girl. Pity. You should have maned up and took your death then." I told him.

"I am not afraid of you. You are not the Queen." He sneered out.

My eyes burned with the white taking over. My gold hair reached down to the tip of my claws. I was glowing in an already bright room. And it snagged the attention of Tarrine. "You were misinformed. I am the Queen of the Light and the Darkness, Amere. And as your Queen, I judge you to life in hell." I told him.

I raised my hand up and stilled him like he did my father. The blade dropped out of his hand and hit the floor. I placed my hand in my pocket and pulled out wood chips from my father's tree. I threw them towards Amere with a gust of wind chasing them. The wood chips hit his body and cuts appeared all over his body. He screamed out as his blood leaked out each deep wound. I pulled the wood chips back into my hand to send them back at Amere with more wind. The wood chips cut deeper into his skin, leaving him holding on by a thread. The wood chips came back to me and this time it formed into a sword.

"For my father," I said and sent the sword directly to his neck. His head went rolling and was stopped by a foot. I threw Amere's body against the wall and walked towards Tarrine. He was staring at me with awe.

"You are beautiful, Queen." He said.

"Who is the Dark Lord that you speak of." I asked.

"You will find out soon enough." He smirked. He kicked the head of Amere towards me. Nylah came out of nowhere and Chun Li kicked that bitch right back at him.

"No, she won't." Nylah said and threw red dust in his eyes. He started screaming and dropped to the ground on his knees.

"I want him." A voice spoke inside of me.

What the fuck? It wasn't my wolf or Chaos. I told her that I was going to do this one on my own since she took out the Southern Facility. I watched as Tarrine tries to teleport from the spot, but he couldn't. Whatever Nylah threw at him had him stuck in this room.

Tyree and Papi walked over to me. "What did you throw on him?"

"It's a reveal dust. His secrets will come to, without any blind spots. Everything that he has been doing will come to light." Nylah told us.

"Please let me have him. I am hungry." The voice spoke again. I frowned my face up and tried to search where the voice was coming from.

"What is wrong Angel?" Papi asked with concern in his voice.

"I hear someone asking me if she can have him. She is begging for him."

"What does she sound like?" Tyree asked as he watched his father writhe in pain. I didn't know how he was doing it. He looked down on his father with pure hate in his eyes.

"She sounds like a child." I told them.

"A child," Nylah asked. Papi walked over to me with his black eyes. He placed his hand on my stomach and felt the magic that was coming through it. He looked up at me with a frown. "Your child is calling to pull the energy from this Guardian." He said. "Why didn't you tell me?" He yelled.

Without warning, Papi went flying back. Tyree backed up from me with wide eyes. "This can't be happening." He whispered. Papi got up and was now standing as a regular Guardian. His eyes were its normal brown color, but a patch of his hair was grey. "Papi," I called out.

"Feed her, Queen. Feed your daughter." He demanded in a tired voice.

I looked at Nylah and she stepped aside. I didn't want to take his energy. I already had Chaos' dark shit inside of me. I didn't need anymore. I hesitated but my daughter felt all the loose energy in the air. I looked back at Papi and it looked like he started sucking in some of the energy. His grey hair became black again and his eyes were back to being black.

"What happened?"

He smiled at me. "I don't think the little one liked me yelling at her Momma. She took my energy through your stomach, Angel."

He told me. He came back over to me and grabbed my hand. "Don't take Papi energy little one. Mommy is about to feed you, all that you need." He whispered and led me to Tarrine. He was still struggling to open his eyes, but he was unsuccessful. Papi reached down, grabbed Tarrine's hand and placed it on my stomach. Tyree and Nylah came forward to protect me in case Tarrine tried something.

"Be careful, Queen," Tyree hissed.

"You don't have to worry young Guardian. Baby girl is not going to let anyone harm her mother. Isn't that right?" Papi spoke looking down at my stomach. Tarrine's energy was sucked out of him right before our eyes in a matter of seconds. His body shriveled up, and his eyes opened with no life left in them.

"*Thank you, Mommy.*" The little voice said.

"You're welcome." I said while placing a hand on my stomach. I felt the changes and how full I became. I also felt stronger and darker. I shook off the feeling and continued talking to her. She sounded like a mature little girl. Nylah and Tyree took a step forward.

"What's next?" Nylah asked.

"We have to torch the bodies before the rogue wolves come feeding on them." Tyree said.

"That won't be a problem." Papi said. He closed his eyes and chanted. The facility started shaking and there was steam coming from the floor. The walls of the facility started sweating and the temperature was going up. Papi was smiling while talking to the greedy child in my stomach. The ground cracked opened and lava came shooting through.

"Really Matteo. You couldn't do this shit while we were standing outside of the building." Tyree yelled.

"You are a Guardian boy. Teleport your ass out here." Papi said. "Let's head back to the house to check on Xavier and your brothers." Tyree grabbed Nylah and disappeared. I thought of home and teleported out the scorched building.

TWENTY-THREE

Matteo

I teleported back to Angel's home. She had a whole lot of explaining to do. She lied to her mate and her brothers. If I would have known the truth, I wouldn't have gone through with her plan. She didn't want another battle close to her home. If she could have prevented the other battle from being at Noel's home, she would have done so.

I appeared in the meeting room with the wolves. Xavier looked like he was ready to go rogue. "Hey Matteo. Tyree and Nylah took Lil Bit. Can you teleport us to where they are?" Dominick rushed over and told me.

"She is fine." I told them. They all were standing staring at me like I lost my mind. "How is it that she is fine, if she is not here?" Xavier asked in a cold voice. His eyes were tinted with blackness. His claws were scratching the table and he was glaring at me with murderous eyes.

"As long as I am breathing, I will not let nothing harm my Angel." I told him.

"But you weren't here Matteo. They took my Godchild." Nico growled out.

Nylah and Tyree walked through the door and all hell broke

loose. Xavier teleported from his chair and was in front of Tyree in no time. "I caught you." Xavier told him. He grabbed Tyree by his neck and tossed him out of the large window. Nylah was about to attack him, but Maxwell attacked her with his claws out. Dom, Nico, and Josh shifted into their wolf and leaped out the window behind Xavier. Josh and Xander walked out the door and stood around the circle that had been made.

"Stop this, Maxwell. I would never hurt the Queen." Nylah told Maxwell as she fought him off.

"Fuck you, you lying bitch. Where is my sister?" He roared out.

"She is telling the truth Maxwell. It was Angel's plan all along." I told him. He didn't hear me. He swiped his hand over Nylah's face. Three long scratch marks appeared on her face. I held my hand up and a small grey ball hit Maxwell in the chest. He hit the floor with the shakes.

"How can you help her after what they did? They took Lil Bit to the Western Facility." He chattered.

I walked over to him and held my hand out. He reached for it and the shakes stopped. "Do you think I would help anyone that had bad intentions towards my baby." I told him. He looked me in the eyes and saw that I was telling the truth. He glanced over at Nylah and saw that her face was already healing from the marks.

"Nylah," he said.

"Don't worry about it, Maxwell. I know how much you love your sister." She told him. "I guess this was to get back at me from last night." She pointed to her face.

I walked off from their little make-up session. I went outside and saw that all of the wolves in each pack was surrounding Xavier and Tyree. I didn't want to fight through the circle, so I teleported in the middle of it. Xavier was staring at Tyree with black eyes. His bone structure was off a little. That means his rogue wolf was coming through. "Xavier, listen to me. Queen is fine. Tyree took her to the facility where all the Supremes and council members were going to be. That was the plan and it worked. We killed them all." I told him.

Xavier was looking through me. He was too far gone to hear anything that I was saying. His movement was fast and swift. He was in front of a surprised Tyree, and uppercut him further in the woods. Xavier's head leaned back and howled out. All the other wolves began to howl with him. He shifted into his wolf and stormed into the woods.

I wasn't about to referee this bullshit. Maxwell and Nylah walked out of the station side by side. "Maxi, I thought you were going to take care of her." Xavion snarled. Maxwell jumped in front of her. "It is not what we thought." He told his brothers. "Lil Bit is ok. She has a lot of explaining to do, though." Maxwell told them.

"Oh shit, we gotta stop Xavier before he kills Tyree." Xander said and took off in the direction the wolves went. I followed behind them. When I reached the spot where they were, I saw that Tyree was now on his feet. He had four claw marks on his chest and one scar on his face. He threw a lightning ball at Xavier. Xavier caught it and threw it back at him with a little of his own magic. Tyree dodged it and pulled the vines from the earth. They wrapped around Xavier and pulled him down. Xavier shifted back into the man.

"I am telling you the truth. I didn't harm the Queen." Tyree was still trying to talk a messed-up Xavier down. Xavier sneered at Tyree's comment and started tearing through the vines. He stood taller and bigger.

"Where is my Queen?" He said deadly in a rattled voice.

"I am here Alpha." Angel's voice came through the crowd. Xavier's head snapped in the direction of her voice. The wolves and men parted and let their Queen through. Dom and the rest of them shifted back and stared at her. She was glowing still with her golden hair and white eyes.

Maxwell and Nylah came through the circle with Xander and Josh. "If you are not of our blood, leave now." Dominick spoked with power. Xavier stood and glared at Angel. I wasn't going to interfere this time. She had to learn to trust her mate, just like he learned to trust her.

When family was the only ones that stood around, Dominick began to yell. "What were you thinking? Or were you thinking? You had us worried out of our fucking mind."

"I did what I had to do, to save my family." She spoke softly.

"Save us." Xavier whispered. He took three steps and was in front of Angel. He wrapped his hand around her throat and pulled her face towards him. "SAVE US! DO IT LOOK LIKE I'M SAVED!" He yelled in her face. His eyes became wild and his grip looked like it was getting tighter around her neck. "You thought that you were saving me, by putting yourself in danger with two mutha-fuckers, that I don't know, to protect you." He said through clenched teeth.

Angel's eyes closed. She turned back into the sweet young lady that they all loved. When she opened her eyes, she stared up at him with love. She placed her hand on the one that was around her throat. "You didn't see what I saw, Alpha. I saw your death, along with our brothers and their mates. I saw Ma'vere feeding off your flesh. I watched as the blood of my family seeped through the floor of my parents' home. So, yes. I saved you and the rest of my fami-ly." She said with tears running down her face. "You're mad and that is understandable. I rather have you here mad at me, than to not have any of you at all." She said softly.

Xavier pushed her away and growled. "DO YOU THINK THAT I CAN LIVE WITHOUT YOU! LOOK AT ME!" Xavier roared. He looked like he was suffering.

Angel held her head down and whispered softly, "You didn't see what I saw."

"Show us what you saw, Lil Bit." Dominick asked.

Angel shook her head with tears still rolling down her face. Xavier got back in her face with a menacing growl. "Show us. And don't make me ask you again."

Angel's eyes opened, and they were red. She held her hand up and a picture appeared in front of us. It was the vision that Nylah showed us before. They saw how Ma'vere fed off their bodies and drained their blood. They saw their Queen on the ground dried up of her energy as the Dark Lord made her watch her family die." Angel closed her eyes and the vision dissipated.

Xavier turned and looked at her. He was back to his normal self, but you could see that he was still angry. "Is there something else you want to tell me."

She nodded her head and grabbed his hand. She placed his hand on her stomach and closed her eyes. "Talk to him." She whispered.

Xavier's face frowned. He didn't know what was about to happen. His expression changed after he heard the little voice of his daughter. Angel was looking up at him smiling. He removed his hand from her stomach and stepped aside. "Let me see." He demanded. I watched in wonder as Xavion floated to them. "AHH, what the hell?" He asked. Everyone mouth was dropped open.

"Put your hand on her stomach." Xavier told him. Xavion looked skeptical and didn't know what to expect. "Trust me brother." Xavier said to him.

Xavion placed his hand on her stomach. We all waited for whatever to happen. Xavion smiled and looked up at Xavier. "Are you serious right now?" He asked with admiration.

"What is going on?" Dom asked them.

Xavion closed his eyes with Angel. He started breathing heavy and his body started sweating. "For real, man, what's going on?" Xander asked this time.

"Give us a minute, Xander." Xavier answered.

Angel opened her eyes and placed her hand on Xavion's face. She tilted it up and pressed his mouth to open. A black cloud came shooting out his mouth and into the air. Angel threw an air bubble into the air to capture it. "Papi, can you take that and bring it home with us. We need to find out who was responsible for that hex." She asked.

"No problem, Angel." I responded.

Xavion let out a deep breath. He looked over at his brothers and smiled. Xavion removed his hand from Angel's stomach. He kneeled before her and raised up her shirt. He placed small kisses on her stomach. "Thank you, Princess. I can't wait to meet you." He said and stood.

"What happened?" Josh asked this time.

"Queen is pregnant with a very gifted baby girl. She told me not to be upset about what happened, because she wasn't going to let anyone harm her mother. I told her that she was just a baby. She told me that she can fix her Uncle Xavion. I told her to show me, and she just did." He said with awe.

"Wait a damn minute. We asked you were you pregnant. You sat yo ass at that table and lied to us." Maxi said.

"I didn't want you guys to sit me out the battle." She said softly.

"Yeah, but you should have told me." Xavier said.

"I'm sorry, King." She stared up at him.

"I know," he said with understanding. They kissed and hugged each other. I shook my head in disgust. This was something I didn't want to see. I took some of the hex smoke and transported to the house.

I let them have their moment but there was something in that vision that I had to check out. The shadow had a face to it. It was Lord Odom. He was going to revive Ma'vere. If that was the case, we were going to need some more help. I knew the right person for the job.

TWENTY-FOUR

Patience

I was standing by the tree waiting for my brothers. They were still upset about how I did things, but I was ok with that. Papi told me that he had to go away for a couple of days and was bringing me back a surprise. I hoped that it was some chocolate. I had been craving that lately.

Xavier didn't want me going anywhere by myself. We told Nanny that I was pregnant and she almost fainted. When she woke up, she cussed my ass out and told me not to do anything so careless again. I promised them all that it wouldn't happen again.

Xavier has been bonding with our Princess every night. They have their own conversation sometimes without me knowing. That was good and all, but I hated when he popped up and demanded shit for me to do. Like, sit all day without getting up. He was worse than Dom. Jessica was always laughing at me. She just didn't know that her ass and Loreen was next. Xavion went home and didn't come out for two days. He was locked up in there with Loreen. He was ready for the mating ceremony, but something was still off about his situation. I told him that I was going to look more into it after Ms. Robin and Nico's ceremony.

I heard my loud ass brothers coming through the woods. I

turned around and looked over at the other tree that was next to my father's. "They are here, King. You can go now." I said. He walked from behind the tree shaking his head.

"Bring your ass home after this. You understand." He said.

"Oh, you don't have to worry about that. We are going to walk her ass home, personally." Dom came through and said. Xavier nodded his head and walked towards me. He pulled me into a kiss and walked off. "What yo lying ass want?" Maxi said. He was extra mad at me. I used his mate that he didn't want, in my plan. I apologized to him every time I saw him. He brushed me off as if he didn't hear anything that I was saying.

"Maxi, please forgive me. How many times do I have to say I'm sorry." I told him with a pout.

"That is not going to work, Lil Bit. Get on with whatever you called us out here for." He said and leaned against the tree. Dom and Josh shook their heads and stood next to me.

"What's up Lil Bit." Josh said and placed his hand on my stomach. "Hey Uncle baby."

"I'm hungry Uncle Josh." She said.

Josh looked up at me with a frown. "When was the last time you ate?"

"I ate two hours ago." I told him and slapped his hand from my stomach.

"You better stop playing with my niece and feed her." He responded.

Dom looked down at me and was about to put his hand on my stomach. I dodged his touch and let out a sigh. "You guys, she only does that when y'all are around. Nanny just made me some BBQ ribs with potato salad, baked macaroni, peas, and a big piece of German chocolate cake. I am full." I told them.

"Eat some more then." Dom mumbled. I ignored him and walked to the tree.

"I told y'all about the tree in Texas and Aunt Lurita told me that she took my mom's ashes and spread them there. When I came to this trail with the girls, this tree called out to me and I didn't know why. I also didn't understand why I couldn't get visions of Daddy.

When I met up with Chaos, she showed me what she did with Daddy ashes." I turned and faced the tree. "She planted his ashes here." I told them.

Dom walked forward and placed his hand on the tree. "We wondered where his body was. And it was here the whole time." He whispered. Josh stood next to him and placed his hand on it as well. Maxi was already leaning on it.

"Daddy," I called out. "I brought your boys to you."

I removed my hand from the tree. They were looking up at the tree with sad eyes. "We miss you Pops." Dom said in a trembling voice. They were all on the verge of crying. I sat and watched them talk to the tree. They laughed out loud and Maxi wiped his face of the tears. He turned towards me with a sad smile. "I forgive you," he told me. I walked over to him and gave him a big hug. He kissed me on the top of my head and didn't let me go. This was one of the best moments in my life.

The Dark Lord

"My Lord, the Western Facility has been destroyed. There were no bodies or energy there." A dark Guardian spoke.

The Dark Lord sat on his throne feeding his rogue wolves left-over body parts. "And what of Tarrine." He said in an old groggily voice.

"We didn't see anyone there. We felt that his magic was used there. We can't find any evidence of his body being there." Another dark Guardian spoke.

"Nesida's child is stronger than I thought. We will have to go to the other facilities and get the other Guardians' energy. Two Supremes should put me back on my feet so that I can get the magic that I need to revive Ma'vere and kill their Queen." He said.

"I thought you needed her energy to do that my Lord."

"No, I can't use her energy. It is no longer pure. She has mated with that dog and it has tainted her blood. The spell said that I need a pure dark Guardian's energy to retrieve the Devil's magic." Dark Lord answered.

"But there are many dark male Guardians, Sire. Pure ones at the nursery in the other facility"

"I wish it was that simple. I need a pure dark female Guardian."
He murmured. "I need the child of their Queen of the Guardians."

Matteo

I didn't understand why her ass moved all the way out here. It took me two and a half days of my energy to get here. Scotland was the perfect place for and an Elemental. Green land, mountains, rocks, water and all that other good shit. She always talked about coming here with the kids or her grandchildren.

I walked up to a small cabin and heard voices. "Mom, you know that you don't need that much salt in that soup."

"I put what I want in it. It's not like you eating." She replied.

"Mom, please stop with the salt; you are going to get high blood pressure." Another voice spoke. I stood by the door and listened to my baby girls talk to their mother. It has been so long since I heard their voices. I wiped my eyes and raised my hand to knock.

"Come on in here, Matteo. The door is already open." Hope's voice came through the door. I twisted the knob and walked into her home. It was a big wide room with small furniture that filled it up. I saw her standing at the stove, making a very salty soup according to the girls.

"Why are you here?" She asked without turning around. I looked over at the table to see if the girls were still there. It was empty. I walked further into the kitchen and sat down in the chair.

"How are you, Hope?" I asked.

She turned around and her beauty had me mesmerized. "Why are you here?" She ignored and asked me again.

"I need your help, Hope."

"I ain't helping you with shit. Get out of my house Matteo." She said and turned around.

"Lord Odom is back. He had been trying to capture your granddaughter and drain her of her energy so that he can bring Ma'vere back." I told her. When she heard Ma'vere's name, her body went still. "Lord Odom needs a pure-blood dark Guardian for that. As you know, she has mated with an Alpha wolf and is now pregnant with our great-granddaughter. They are planning on killing them both. I won't be able to protect them from Lord Odom and Ma'vere alone, Hope. Will you come back home and help your Patience and her baby girl." The fire on the stove rose and the wind outside started knocking on the window. The water that was dripping from the sink, turned to ice. Hope's beautiful mahogany brown hair became lighter.

"They are coming for my granddaughter babies." She said in a gentle voice.

"Yes," I answered. She turned around with her black eyes glaring at me.

"That is something that I will not allow." Hope said with a sinister smile.

To be continued...